The Missing Model

ALSO BY ROGER SILVERWOOD

YORKSHIRE MURDER MYSTERIES
Book 1: The Missing Nurse
Book 2: The Missing Wife
Book 3: The Man in the Pink Suit
Book 4: The Morals of a Murderer
Book 5: The Auction Murders
Book 6: The Missing Killer
Book 7: The Umbrella Murders
Book 8: The Missing Millionaire
Book 9: The Missing Thief
Book 10: Find the Lady
Book 11: The Missing Model
Book 12: Murder in Bare Feet
Book 13: The Missing Husband
Book 14: The Cuckoo Clock Murders
Book 15: Shrine to Murder
Book 16: The Snuffbox Murders
Book 17: The Dog Collar Murders
Book 18: The Cheshire Cat Murders
Book 19: The Diamond Rosary Murders
Book 20: Thirteen Steps to Murder
Book 21: The Fruit Gum Murders
Book 22: The Money Tree Murders
Book 23: Angel and the Actress
Book 24: The Murder List
Book 25: The Lipstick Murders
Book 26: The Music Box Murders
Book 27: Murder on Time
Book 28: Angel's Final Problem?
Book 29: Angel and the Nun

STANDALONE
The Guilty Daughter

The
MISSING
MODEL

ROGER SILVERWOOD

JOFFE BOOKS

Revised edition 2025
Joffe Books, London
www.joffebooks.com

First published as *The Wigmaker* in Great Britain in 2008

This paperback edition was first published
in Great Britain in 2025

Cover art by Nick Castle

ISBN: 978-1-80573-189-4

ONE

Sheffield City Centre, South Yorkshire, UK
Easter Sunday, 8th April, 2 a.m.

The sky was as black as a judge's cap.

A man with a bag strapped to his back scrambled up a drainpipe on the side of a furniture shop to the second storey roof. He lifted himself up from the gutter, straightened his arms, swung himself on to the tiles and then scampered up to the apex of the roof. He picked his steps like a tightrope walker across it to the adjoining building, where he squatted astride the apex and began to unseat one of the blue slate tiles. It soon gave way. It had not been touched since it was built ninety years earlier. He placed the tile safely inside his jacket, then he tore at the next one until he had eight slates safely inside his coat. He had made a hole large enough for him, with the slates and the backpack, to get through. He shone a torch down inside to see how far he had to drop. It was about a twelve-foot drop on to cross beams about fifteen feet apart. He took a three-pronged hook out of his backpack, fastened a pulley to it, secured the hook round the apex coving, threaded a rope through the pulley, then, holding both

1

ropes, he lowered himself down into the loft of the furniture shop. He landed quietly on the beams and left the rope hanging there. He placed the slates from inside his jacket tidily in a pile on a crossbeam; he hadn't wanted to risk them clattering down the furniture-shop roof and smashing on to the pavement below. He wiped his mouth with the back of his gloved hand. Then he flashed the torch around. It was, as he had expected, a dusty, unpleasant place, with more than its fair share of cobwebs. He put a hand into his inside pocket and took out a mask. It was a plastic face mask of a fox. He put it on and fitted the elastic over the back of his big shock of red hair: there was no knowing when he might come across a CCTV camera, perhaps one with a night lens. He crossed the loft in the direction of the beams underfoot to a rough door in an even rougher brick wall. He heaved at the door and it gave way easily. It had been there since the building was first built and had probably never been inspected or even looked at since. He flashed the torch around. He was looking for a loft cover into the floor below. There should be one. There was always one, sometimes several. He found it. It was about a yard square and made up of tongue-and-grooved five-by-one timber. He sighed with relief, crossed to it, crouched down, took out another three-pronged hook, dug it into a nearby beam, fastened on a pulley, threaded another rope through. He was ready for a second descent. He lifted the loft cover away, it weighed very little, then listened. He shone the torch down into the office below. As expected, the building was deserted and in darkness. He sat on the edge of the opening, his feet hanging down into the room. He put the torch between his teeth, took hold of both ropes and lowered himself through the hole.

He was safely inside the jeweller's shop.

* * *

2

Forest Hill Estate, Bromersley, South Yorkshire, UK
Tuesday, 10 April 2007, 7 a.m.

It was 7 a.m. Michael Angel was busily munching muesli and prunes in his blue-and-white striped pyjamas and red slippers while Mary, his wife, returned from the front door of 30 Park Street, a semi-detached bungalow on the Forest Hill estate. She had a copy of the local newspaper, the *Bromersley Chronicle* in her hand. She opened it up. The headline jumped out at her.

'Oooo!' She gasped. 'You'll never guess, Michael,' she muttered, sitting down, pulling up to the little kitchen table and staring at the paper.

'What?' he said, being careful not to spray the muesli around.

'Smith and Glogowsky's shop in Sheffield has been robbed! Big page spread. Listen to this.'

Angel *was* surprised. His eyes opened wide. He was about to say something. She beat him to it.

'Here, listen.'

She read:

THE FOX IN £4.5M JEWEL HEIST

Smith & Glogowsky, the famous jeweller's shop in the centre of Sheffield was broken into and robbed by The Fox. Gold jewellery set with precious stones including diamonds, rubies and emeralds were taken, including an all-diamond tiara being reset for Lady Tiverton of Bromersley.

The robbery took place over the Easter holiday weekend.

The opening of the safes and sorting of the jewels took place in front of CCTV cameras with night lenses, so the activities of the daring thief known as The Fox were fully recorded. It showed a man with a lot of hair believed to be ginger and wearing the mask of a fox.

It was reported that The Fox only took jewellery set in platinum and 18ct gold or better, which inevitably included the largest and best precious stones, which Smith & Glogowsky had in stock. It happened over the holiday period when the shop was closed for three days. Police say that The Fox had gained entrance through the roof of the neighbouring premises, then crossed the shared loft, where he dropped down into an office, opened the alarm-box controls and, it is thought, squirted two aerated chemicals which on contact with each other became instant setting glue which prevented the alarm system operating. Industrial chemists and security experts are said to be working non-stop to try to discover the exact process.

The proprietor Mr Igor Glogowsky is reported to be 'stunned' by the robbery. He is said to have understood that the alarm system was infallible. Whilst entirely covered by insurance, he said, some of the items were irreplaceable.

This holiday robbery was the twenty-second robbery by The Fox using the same MO. The police have made no progress in identifying and apprehending the thief. He was assumed to be a local man, who worked alone. Most of the robberies had been committed in Yorkshire, but there had also been cases in other parts of the country as far north as Newcastle upon Tyne. In four years, he has robbed more than twenty-two jewellery shops and the police admit to being completely baffled by the case.

Even in these sophisticated days of DNA, it seemed that there had never been any kind of substance, human fluid or matter or hair left behind at the scene or anywhere else that could be attributed to him.

Every policeman in the UK was desperate to unmask and arrest him. Profilers at all levels had been making *projections, but with such limited information their reports had not proved adequate.*

The general public is requested to report anything suspicious that they may have seen in or around the shop over the holiday period to any police officer.

Each of the 43 forces, as well as the Serious Organized Crime Agency (SOCA), have been put on special watch for this master serial jewellery thief known as 'The Fox'.

She folded the paper. 'What do you think to that?'

Angel shook his head.

It was bad news for policemen, there was no denying it.

'The newspapers will have a field day, Mary,' he said. 'Whenever The Fox strikes, the press, particularly the tabloids, fill their pages with every detail of the latest crime and compare it with the earlier ones attributed to him, and gleefully publish cartoons and all sorts of tales ridiculing the police. I feel sorry for the Sheffield lads. This Fox chap makes them look like mugs, which they are not.'

'The Fox must be somebody round here.'

'Aye, he must be,' he said. 'Oh! Look at the time.'

* * *

Flat 4, Jubilee Close, Bromersley
Friday, 13 April 2007, 9.30 p.m.

Zoe Grainger was on her own in the tiny, cramped kitchen, pressing a skirt on a skeletal ironing table squeezed awkwardly between the sink unit and the little kitchen table because of the limited length of the cord on the iron. She was concentrating on making the pleat in the skirt look tidy and smart, when suddenly something occurred to her. She put the hot iron on the stand, rushed into the little sitting room and looked around. She was looking for her hand-bag. It was on the sideboard. She grabbed it and felt around inside it. She took out a powder compact. She snapped it open and looked at her eyes and face in the mirror. She moved around a bit to get the best light and to see all her face. She wrinkled her nose and shook her head. Zoe knew she had a great figure, long shapely legs, round bottom, slim waist and a big perky bosom. Her jet-black hair was thick and manageable, and much admired. She didn't have need to tint it or do much at all with it. Even her voice, once described by a sexy man on the deli counter in Tesco's as gravelly, she wouldn't have changed. But she reckoned her face let her down. She had thought for some time that if she could have had a smaller, narrower and slightly turned-up nose, and less distance between her nose and her top lip, she could have had a more than equal chance of pulling any man she fancied. However, plastic surgery was expensive and not available to her, nor ever likely to be.

She quickly snapped shut the compact and tossed it into her handbag, then glanced up at the bigger mirror over the clock. She unfastened the second button down on her blouse and pulled it tight to show a bit more skin. She smirked at the mirror. It exposed the smallest amount of cleavage, by today's standards quite unremarkable. She smiled into the mirror, nodded and turned away. Then she stopped thoughtfully, scowled, turned back, fastened the button and checked it was tidy. As she did so she thought she caught sight of a hair or two out of place. She began to fiddle with them. She heard a noise on the stairs . . . rushed back into the kitchen, and had her hand on the iron as the stairs door opened.

A tall, slim, sun-tanned young man, with blue eyes, dark hair and muscles as tight as a moneylender's contract, swaggered into the little kitchen. He was looking pleased with himself. He flashed a smile at her as she stood at the ironing board, still running the iron over her skirt.

'Hi, sweetheart. Got me a clean shirt?'

Her eyes flashed and her lips quivered. 'You're not going out?'

'Yes. Yes. I'm going out,' he said, his face tightening. 'Why would I want a clean shirt if I wasn't going out?'

'Where you going?'

'*You* can't come.'

'Why not?'

His blue eyes flashed angrily. 'It's business.'

She snatchily rearranged the skirt on the ironing board and banged the iron on to it. 'I could come and wait, and we could go on somewhere, have a drink? Make a change.'

'Naw. Where's my shirt?'

She turned the skirt over, licked her lips and said, 'Who was that on the phone?'

'Nobody. Now can I have a shirt?'

She lifted up the skirt, put it on a hanger and hung it on a knob on the cupboard door. 'It *was* a woman, wasn't it?' she said quietly.

'No. It wasn't.'

'Sounded like a woman.'

'You couldn't possibly have heard, but, as a matter of fact, it was a man offering me a job.'

'At this god-forsaken time on a Friday night? You must think I fell out of a tree.'

'A job. Work. Money, Zoe.'

'Huh.'

'I've told you it would happen. Big money. I've told you.'

'Huh.'

'I told you,' he said. He had to convince her. 'I'm getting on really well with this man. He's well-to-do. *Very* well-to-do. And great connections. This is the opportunity I've been waiting for, Zoe. Now will you tell me where there's a clean bloody shirt or do I have to go out in my vest?'

'Huh. It's funny time to be interviewing a man . . . Friday night at half past nine.'

'Not an interview. I had the interview last week. He's going to tell me what he wants me to do. He's an important man. He works all hours.'

'What's his name?'

'Ah. I can't tell you his name. It's sort of . . . hush-hush.'

'A government job?'

'Yes. You could say that. Sort of undercover . . . for the police.'

He had fallen straight into her trap. She knew her husband so well.

'Pull the other one.'

'Well, not the police exactly, but it's . . . confidential. You never believe me.'

'Huh! It's another woman. I knew it. I always knew that you had to have a bit of cheap skirt on the side!'

'Are you going to give me a clean shirt or not? I shall be late.'

'Where are you meeting her?'

'It's a *man*! He's going to tell me what he wants me to do.'

'Whereabouts are you meeting *him* then, Gabriel?'

'I can't say.'

'In a pub? Is it the Fat Duck?'

'It isn't in a pub.'

The phone rang.

They looked at each other. Eyebrows raised. Neither of them expected a call at that time.

'Could be him,' he said.

He reached out for it. 'Hello, yes?' he said tentatively.

Zoe could hear faintly a distorted voice through the earpiece, but she couldn't detect what was being said.

He looked across at her, his blue eyes looked overjoyed. He tried to convey the happiness to her. Into the mouthpiece, he said, 'Gabriel Grainger, yes . . . For how long? . . . Oh? Right. No, I'm not busy with anything else . . . Thank you. Thank you very much. You won't regret it . . . Ten minutes? I'll be right there . . . Goodbye.'

He replaced the phone. 'That was him. There you are, *now* do you believe me?' he said, his eyes shining. 'I've got to leave straightaway. Throw a few things in a suitcase, he said. There's money in this, Zoe. Big money. Can't you believe me, this time? Trust me.'

'I've trusted you before. You're a born liar. I should never have married you. It was for better or worse. It's always been worse. Where are you going to?'

'I don't know exactly, but it will be OK. I'll be back before you know it.'

He reached over the ironing board, grabbed her tightly by the shoulders, gave her a hurried, rough kiss on the mouth and said, 'This is it, Zoe. My chance to hit the big money. Have faith in me, for once, you silly cow.'

He let her go.

She turned away. She pretended the kiss had had no effect on her. She loved him too much. She couldn't let him see that. She knew he was making a fool of her. She wanted to murder him, but if she had done, she would have cried after him for the rest of her life.

'Where's that shirt?'

That brought her back to earth. Without a change of expression, she reached into the linen basket, dug around and pulled out a shirt.

He snatched it, grinned and dashed off.

She watched him rush out of the kitchen and listened to him clump up the stairs. She sighed, rubbed her nose with the back of her hand, sniffed, turned to the linen basket, dragged out a pillowcase, and draped it across the ironing board.

* * *

Heathrow Airport Concourse
Sunday, 29 April 2007, 3 p.m.

'Still no sign of the bitch?'

'No, Max. I told you, she might be making her own way here.'

'Wanna bet? And buy her own ticket? You must be joking. Anyway the arrangement was clear. It was to meet here at two o' clock. I have done this with her a few times. She knows exactly where to meet us. And she's got my mobile number. If she had a problem, she could phone. Have you got the number of that agency?'

'It's in my book. Here, hold the camera. Don't put it down anywhere. Too many thieving bastards around.'

'What's the number? What's the frigging number?'

'I'm getting it. I'm getting it. I'll dial it.'

'Hurry up. Hurry up.'

'It's ringing out. There.'

Max Peppino hurriedly exchanged the camera for the mobile phone.

There was a click and the phone was answered.

'Top Notch Model Agency, twenty-four seven. Melanie speaking, can I help you?'

'Max Peppino here, darling. I'm on the concourse at Heathrow and I'm bloody fed up. Katrina hasn't shown.'

'Really? Oh. Good afternoon, Mr Peppino. Katrina? Oh dear. I'm very surprised. She's usually so reliable, I don't know what to say. She's not phoned you? Is your mobile working all right?'

'Perfectly. Now we've missed the two o'clock flight because she didn't show. I've the chance of three seats on the 1640 flight, but she'll have to be here by four o'clock or we won't get on.'

'I'm very sorry, Mr Peppino. I don't understand it. Have you tried to phone her?'

' 'Course I have. And her home number. I can't raise her.'

'Oh dear. I am so sorry. I can't think what may have happened. She never misses an assignment. And she's never late. And she loves going on shoots with you. And I know she was so looking forward to it. I suppose I *might* be able to get you a replacement. There's Mary Ann, who is coming up very quickly, but it's extremely short notice.'

'Look, Melanie, if I'd merely wanted a long-legged blonde with big Bristols, I could have sailed round Kings Cross in my Jag and had a choice of a dozen for peanuts. I want Katrina. Her face is known. I paid top whack for her, and that's who I want. For the money I'm paying her, she should be here, on time, with her engine running. I want Katrina, not just any old body. If she's not here in twenty minutes, in time to catch the four o'clock flight, the deal is off and I'll be suing you.

This cock-up is costing me about twelve hundred a day, so you'd better dust your cheque book off.'

Melanie's voice hardened. 'I am extremely sorry, Mr Peppino, that you have been inconvenienced by Katrina's failure to arrive on time. I expect she is still trying to reach you. If not, something calamitous must have happened, which concerns me greatly. If she does not arrive, you will obviously not be billed. I have offered you a substitute and I regret there is nothing else I can do. As for compensation, I suggest you reread your agreement. You will see that we are not responsible for any illness, accidents or matters of any kind that are out of our control. Now is there any other way in which I can help you?'

Max Peppino didn't answer. He knew that if he had he would have been too offensive. He closed the phone, bit his lip and handed it back to the man holding the camera.

TWO

It was 7.35 a.m.

There was a noise from the hall.

'Postman,' Mary said.

She put down her toast, got up from the table and went out.

There were four envelopes in the post that morning. She reached for her spectacles, and frowned as she sorted through them, placed three in front of her husband, but held one back, took a knife from the breakfast table and slit it open.

Michael Angel looked up interestedly. Mary didn't get much post and when she did, it was usually from her side of the family or someone trying to sell her something. This appeared to fall into neither category.

'Who's it from?'

'Don't know yet,' she muttered eager to get at the contents.

The envelope contained an A4 sheet. She quickly unfolded it. It was a letter with a cheque attached.

'It's from some solicitors.'

He blinked. 'A solicitor's letter? What you been up to?' he said wryly. He saw the cheque and frowned.

'Solicitors in London,' she said. 'Black, Michaels and Hope.'

'Sound like something kids have for breakfast with milk on. What do they want?'

She didn't reply. She read the letter quickly.

Angel was curious. 'What do they want?'

She looked up at him and beamed. 'I've been left some money.'

He blinked. That was a pleasant surprise. Came at a good time too, he thought.

'Do you remember me telling you about Great-Uncle John who went out to India for ICI?'

'You said HMV,' he said accusingly.

'Same thing,' she said, pulling an impatient face.

Angel's mouth dropped open. When he had swallowed he said, 'Vaguely. What about him?'

'He died, poor lamb. But he left all his great nephews and nieces, of whom I am one, a bequest.'

'Great. How much?'

She smiled at him and said, 'After tax and conversion from Australian dollars to English sterling, divided among the six of us it comes to six hundred and six pounds.'

Angel began to tear into his post. He looked up. 'Gas bill,' he muttered. 'That six hundred and six will more than clear that.'

'Not likely,' she said.

His face brightened. 'We can have an extra few days in Scotland.'

She shook her head. 'No. I don't like Scotland anyway. It's you that likes the place. No,' she said dreamily. 'I am going to get something I like . . . something that I've always wanted.'

'A new outfit?' he said.

Her eyes lit up. 'No,' she said firmly. 'I've always wanted a really classy table for the hall. I shall get this into the bank and keep my eyes open for one.'

Angel's jaw dropped. 'For six hundred quid you could furnish an entire house. Besides, there's no room for it.'

'Something antique . . . like Chippendale.'

'Chippendale!' he bawled. 'You'll be lucky to get a pair of Chippendale chopsticks for six hundred quid.'

'A small occasional table . . . but it's got to be Chippendale or Hepplewhite.'

'Where did you get all those expensive-sounding names from?' he said tearing into his letters.

'The women's circle had a man talking on antique furniture only last Tuesday.'

Angel grunted as he tore into another envelope. 'Look, we can get thirty-five per cent off a motorized wheelchair. Doesn't say how much they are in the first place.'

'Who wants a motorized wheelchair? Tomorrow we are going on a visit to Seymour Timms just outside Harrogate. World expert on the growing of chrysanthemums. Have you heard of him?'

'Mmm. Might have. He must be getting on.'

'Was on the BBC gardening programmes years ago.'

'Great. Hope you enjoy it, love.'

Angel tore into the last envelope. There was something bright and colourful inside. 'Look, I've a voucher for twelve thousand pounds. All I have to do is phone this number and run up a gigantic phone bill to find out that I haven't won twelve thousand pounds, I've won a table mat made in China worth four p.'

'You ought to be doing something about that sharp practice, Michael. You're in a good position to deal with crooks like that.'

'They slip through our fingers as easily as your jelly, Mary. Oh! Look at the time!'

* * *

Detective Inspector Angel arrived at his office, took off his raincoat and hung it on the hook on the stationery cupboard. He glanced at the pile of envelopes and paperwork on his desk and wrinkled his nose. He was about to start fingering through it when the phone rang. He leaned over and picked up the handset. It was his boss, Detective Superintendent Harker. He could tell by the loud and noisy breathing. The man had asthma and every other ailment heard of.

'Come up here, lad, smartish,' he growled. There was a click and the line went dead.

Angel wrinkled his nose and both corners of his mouth turned down. Driving in, he had been feeling quite chipper, particularly in view of Mary's unexpected inheritance from down under. He replaced the phone, closed the office door and made for the green corridor. He did a mental stocktake on matters outstanding as he strode up to the boss's office. Last night, he had finished all the paperwork on his latest murder case . . . about a man posing as someone else and then murdering his wife . . . and passed it all on a plate to the CPS. He thought that getting a guilty verdict would be as easy as pie for Mr Twelvetrees, the barrister. Angel knew he was a bit behind with some of the routine statistics but, if he had an uninterrupted run, he expected to catch up with them by the weekend.

He arrived at the superintendent's office. He knocked on the door and walked in.

Harker looked up from the desk. His head was like a turnip. He was wiping his nose. It was the size and shape of a Victorian mixer tap. 'Aye. Come in.'

Angel could smell the TCP. Harker frequently smelled of the stuff. His nose was red. He'd got a real corker of a summer cold.

Angel made for a chair.

'You needn't sit down, lad.'

Angel looked at him. 'Got a call from the duty officer, fire department. They were summoned to a blaze at 38 Market Street at 0600 hours. Flames shooting out of the roof. It's a shop of some sort. Only small. The man said it was a wig factory. Didn't know there were such places. I suppose they've got to make them smelly things somewhere. Anyway, Peter Wolff, the proprietor, he was found dead in the shop. Take it from there.'

'Right, sir.'

* * *

Angel pulled up behind two fire engines, a white van that he recognized as the forensic van and Dr Mac's car. They were parked outside a small shop squashed into a long row of other shops up a side street on the edge of the main shopping centre of Bromersley. A few shoppers and people with nothing better to do were standing around and staring at the dark, miserable little burnt-out shop and the official vehicles parked in front of it. The glass frontage and some of the stonework above it was blackened with soot, but you could just make out the words on the plate-glass window: *Peter Wolff hair stylist and wig maker to the stars.* And below that, *By appointment only* then a phone number. The interior of the shop was dark, there were no lights and no indication as to the activity inside.

Angel got out of the car to see a man in white overalls, boots and cap come out of the shop door carrying a roll of tape. He began to feed out *DO NOT CROSS — POLICE LINE* tape across the front of the shop door. Angel recognized him. It was DS Taylor. He was head of Scene of Crimes Office (SOCO) at Bromersley.

He saw Angel and threw up a sort of salute.

'Good morning, sir,' he said.

Angel nodded. 'What you got, Don?'

'Pretty sure it's murder, sir. A man, thought to be Peter Wolff, proprietor of the shop, found dead in bed. Shot at close range, I think. Fire started at all three levels. So it's got to be arson. He lived on the top floor . . . not much room.'

'So he actually lived over the shop? Didn't think people did that anymore. Did he live here on his own?'

'Don't know yet, sir. Top floor seems to have been living accommodation, second floor was where he had a sort of office, and where he made the wigs . . . sewed them up . . . stored the hair and the skull caps and so on. The ground floor was the shop where they were fitted and sold.'

He nodded. 'I suppose wigs and hair are highly inflammable. Were there a lot?'

'By the look of the blaze, I dare say.'

'Dr Mac with the body?'

'Yes sir. Top floor.'

'Stairs safe?'

'Yes, sir. Soaking wet. Where there's carpet it'll be slippy.'

Two firemen came through the door and brushed past them; they were each carrying a rolled-up hose. Angel was caught by one of them on the elbow. Water dripped from a crease in his yellow waterproof on to Angel's trouser-leg and shoe. He wrinkled his nose.

The fireman said, 'Sorry, mate.'

Angel shook it off and said, 'Have you finished? Is the fire out and is the building safe?'

'Yes, mate. We're off. The fire is out but you'll need your own surveyor about structural safety. But it looks OK to me. Cheers.'

Angel thanked him and they disappeared behind one of the fire engines. He looked over Taylor's shoulder through the door into the blackness. 'I'm expecting my sergeants Ron Gawber and Trevor Crisp. If you see them, tell them where I am, will you? And I want some gloves.'

'My lads inside have them, sir.'

'Right,' he said and stepped through the door. He wandered through the downstairs shop, swimming in a half-inch of water. He looked at the black and steamed-up wall of mirrors with two sinks and two chairs facing them. On the opposite decorated wall were about twenty framed photographs behind steamed up glass of beautiful women. Angel assumed they were famous actresses or celebrities in flamboyant hairstyles, trying to look enigmatic. Their names were printed underneath, but he didn't recognize any of them. He swished his way through more water to a door in the rear wall. He frowned as he looked back at it. He felt a dribble of water on his head; it ran down his face. He moved quickly.

There was a loo by the back door and a window next to it. A semicircle in the windowpane had been scored round the latch and a piece of glass neatly removed. He nodded knowingly. He had seen it many times before. He wasn't best pleased. It had professional written all over it, which meant that SOCO were unlikely to lift any usable fingerprints around the point of entry or anywhere else.

He retraced his steps, kicked his way through the puddles to the bottom of the stairs and made his way up to the first floor, being careful not to touch the handrail. As he reached the top the smell of a mixture of sulphuretted hydrogen and burning sofa hit his nostrils. Bad as it was, he had smelled worse. A man in whites, holding a flashlight and flicking a brush over a metal filing cabinet heard him approach and turned round. Angel didn't know the man behind the white protective clothes hood and mask.

'Got any gloves?' he said.

The man broke off the dusting for prints and reached down to a large white plastic bag by his side. He fished inside and pulled out a thin white packet and handed it to him.

'Ta,' Angel said. He tore off the top of the packet and took out the gloves. 'When you get downstairs, you'll see the rear window has had a segment scored out of it.'

'I've seen it, sir. Don't worry. I won't miss it. But it's hard to get prints . . . everything covered in soot.'

Angel smiled knowingly. 'Aye. But if there *are* any prints, they would be there before the soot fell. You can blow the soot off with something like an ordinary drinking straw. All right?'

The man's eyebrows shot up. 'Oh yes, sir. Yes.'

The SOCO man seemed surprised at Angel's comment. There was a short pause and the man added, 'Come to think of it, I've got a pipette in the kit, sir.'

Angel turned away from him and shook his head. He looked round the room. It was a black, smelly mess. Almost everything had been destroyed. On the wall by the stairs were lots of smoky cuttings of newspaper ads pinned to the wall with Blu Tack. Angel read one. It was four inches, double column.

It had a photograph of a young woman with a flamboyant hairstyle trying to look beautiful. The photograph was positioned in the middle of the text. Written across the corner in blue ballpoint pen were the words '*Brom Chron 23/5.08.*' It read:

Peter Wolff
Wig maker to the stars
38 Market Street,
Bromersley
Telephone 12574
Wigs, buns, extensions, pieces. All colours and shades, perfectly matched. Hair bought (minimum length 12"). Personal attention. By appointment only.

Angel wrinkled his nose. The ad seemed a bit terse, but no doubt Mr Wolff knew what he was about. Above the cuttings at eye level was a short shelf, crammed with a dozen or more jars, like he remembered seeing in chemists' shops. They had elegant stoppers in them and mysterious labels printed in Latin in gold on black. SOCO would look into them, but he surmised they would be dyes, bleaches and that sort of thing. He turned back into the room. Very little else had survived the flames and water. The workbench, the chair where he assumed Wolff had worked threading and cutting the wigs were black wrecks. In a corner away from where the main seat of the fire had been was a tall metal four-drawer filing cabinet. The green paint was blistered in places. He pulled the rubber gloves on to each hand with a satisfying snap, took a pen out of his pocket, placed it behind the handle of the top drawer and pulled the drawer open. There were files neatly labelled and seemingly in alphabetical order. They were untouched by the fire. That was good. He slammed it shut.

'Great. Is Dr Mac up the next flight?'

'With the body, sir, yes.'

Angel turned round and made his way up the second flight to the top floor.

The top floor seemed to have suffered the least fire damage. There was a bedroom, a bathroom without a bath, a small living room with a small oven in the corner, a worktop, a television and a sink, a settee, an easy chair and a small table. The rooms didn't have doors, just archways.

Dr Mac, a small white-haired Glaswegian in a white paper suit was leaning over a large divan bed. His bag of mysterious surgical instruments stood open on the floor. He turned to see Angel appear through the arch.

'Morning, Mac. What you got?'

'Never been to a wig maker's before,' Mac said slowly in a broad Glaswegian accent you could batter with a haggis.

'No. Neither have I. Is that the man, Peter Wolff?'

'Yes. It's him all right. There's a picture of him in last week's *Bromersley Chronicle*. He won a prize or something for making a wig for some famous popsy or other on the telly.'

'I wouldn't know. But it's good to be sure whose body we are looking at.'

Mac bent down to his bag, permitting Angel from the archway to see the body of a man still in bed, naked to the waist with dried blood on his chest; he had a bald, domed head and ribs sticking out like a turkey carcass on Boxing Day.

'Was he shot?' Angel asked, as he observed the face of the body. It was pasty, thin and white.

'Aye,' the doctor continued. 'One bullet. About a .303. Timing will be a bit difficult. The fire has made a mess of my usual method of calculations.'

Angel nodded. 'But it's reasonable to assume that Wolff was murdered before the fire was started.'

'Aye. That's logical,' the doctor said, sealing up a polythene envelope and writing on the front of it. 'And it's correct.'

'I assume then that the murderer would have broken into the premises, made his way up the two flights of stairs to this floor.' Angel suddenly stopped, frowned, and said, 'Tell me, Mac, has he got any pants on?'

'No,' the doctor said. 'Why?'

'I was thinking, he must have been murdered in bed. No man would normally stay in bed if he heard noises of an intruder in the place. If he were naked, he would certainly have felt vulnerable and further disadvantaged. There appear to be no signs of a struggle in or around the bed. I guess Mr Wolff may have been shot while he was asleep.'

'It's possible. He hasn't been moved since death. I can say that for certain.'

Angel seemed satisfied with that preliminary analysis. He rubbed his chin.

Mac leaned over to the little bedside table and picked up his stand thermometer. He gazed at the level of the mercury. 'You see, Michael. It's still almost sixty in here and the windows are wide open.'

Angel nodded. 'So what time do you estimate death?'

Mac pulled an impatient face. He closed the thermometer case and pushed it into his bag. 'Well, I suppose it would have to be between 2200 hours last night and 0400 hours this morning. It would be difficult to be more accurate than that.'

'Fair enough. The fire was first reported at 0600 hours. Mmm.'

He was getting a clearer picture.

There were footsteps on the stairs and a figure appeared behind him. It was DS Gawber. 'Morning, sir.'

'There you are, Ron. I've about finished here for the moment.' He turned to the doctor. 'I'll wait to hear from you, Mac,' he said.

'Aye. I'll do the PM this afternoon. Don't expect a lot from here. The murderer was clean, tidy and well organized,' the doctor called after him.

Angel wrinkled his nose. He pointed out of the room, Gawber backed out and the two of them moved into the living room area.

'This is murder *and* arson, Ron. I want you to find out Wolff's next of kin, then ask around . . . in the neighbouring shops for any info about him . . . particularly about any regular visitors . . . customers, whatever.'

Suddenly they heard a voice from below them calling out, 'Inspector! Inspector Angel! Are you still up there?'

It was DS Taylor. Angel went to the banister and called back down. 'Yes Don, what is it?'

'Young lady to see you, sir. Friend of Mr Wolff.'

Angel's head went up. That was good news. It might save a lot of shoe leather and time.

'Right, I'll come down.'

'I'll push off, sir,' Gawber said. 'See what I can dig up.' He made for the stairs. Angel followed behind him.

Taylor met Angel at the shop door. 'She's just outside, sir. Didn't let her in. Says she knows Peter Wolff.'

THREE

Angel opened the shop door and a young woman of about twenty-five with a doleful face and beautiful eyes greeted him. She spoke pleasantly, with no smile. She held her head erect and stiff, with her shoulders back. Her hair was shiny, thick and black. She had long slim legs, was about five feet tall and she had a handbag on a strap over her very lean shoulder.

'Is Peter dead?' she murmured, wiping her eyes with a tissue.

Angel nodded. 'I am afraid so, miss. Please come in,' he said, holding open the door for her.

She stepped gingerly into the shop, noticing firstly the water on the floor, then the grimy walls. Her big eyes looked round at the walls and mirrors. Her face reflected how shocked she was at what she now saw.

'You knew him well?'

'As well as anybody, I suppose,' she said. Angel reckoned that her enunciation was exaggerated, indicating that English was not her first language.

'What was your relationship with him, miss?'

'My name is Gina Podolsky. I worked for him now and again. What has happened to him? Please tell me.'

Angel was impressed by the genteel presence of the woman. She kept her head down and her eyes lowered.

'I don't know,' he replied quietly. 'He is dead and the place was set on fire. I am hoping you can help me. What did you do exactly? Were you intending to work for him today?'

Her eyes flashed crossly. She gave a quick jerk at the waist that made her skirt fan out a little way to show more of her legs, she blinked affectedly and said, 'I am a model. I posed for all Peter Wolff's pictures for his catalogue. He said I was the best model he ever had.' Her voice faltered. 'Today, he wanted to shoot me in some new wigs and hairpieces he had made.' She suddenly broke down in tears. 'Oh, this is awful.'

'Take your time, miss,' Angel said gently.

He waited a little while, then he said, 'Did you know him long?'

'Thank you. I am all right, now,' she said, finding a pocket in which to stuff the tissue. 'Three or four years. I live in Sheffield. We had an arrangement . . . a booking. I was to be here today between nine thirty and ten o'clock for around four hours. He was preparing his spring catalogue. It's not a big catalogue, you understand. A sort of glorified leaflet that showed around sixty pictures of me in different wigs. He sends it out to his client list and any enquirers, I suppose.'

'How well did you know him?' Angel said looking closely into her eyes.

There was that flash of anger again. She thought that Angel might be suggesting something improper. She lifted her chin. 'I knew him only as a model for his wigs. Nothing more. He was nearly old enough to be my father, I suppose. But he was a very nice man.'

'Did he have any family? Was he married?'

'I think that he said he had been married but his wife had died. I do not know if they had had any children.'

'I have to find his next of kin, you see, Miss Podolsky.'

'I am sorry. I cannot help you there. I know nothing more about that.'

'Hmm. Have you any idea who might have wanted him dead? Do you know if he had any enemies?'

'Oh no. Peter was one of the nicest men you would wish to meet.'

'Did he have any money troubles . . . as far as you know?'

'I shouldn't have thought so. He always seemed to be busy at the bench. The telephone rang a lot. He only saw customers by appointment. All his wigs, extensions or pieces were individually made to order. He couldn't do with time-wasters coming in and spending half an hour trying on cheap stock wigs as if they were hats, then leaving with something cheap. He said that they wouldn't be satisfied long term. The public would know that they weren't the real thing. You see, he made for the well-heeled who wanted to look good close up. He had quite a few customers in the entertainment business, who always had to look glamorous on the screen. You know the sort of people I mean. Those who haven't time to attend their hairdresser.'

Angel knew what she meant. He wasn't making much headway.

'How did he get his commissions? Ads in magazines?'

'I guess he must get most of his work from the internet. I know he has his own website. I've checked it out.'

Angel nodded. That was the way business was going.

'Did he employ anybody?' he asked.

'No, I don't think so. When I have been here I have only ever seen him with customers.'

There was the ring of a mobile phone. It was Angel's. 'Excuse me,' he said. He turned away from the elegant Miss Podolsky, dived into his pocket, opened the phone and pressed the button. It was Harker.

'Yes, sir.'

'Are you still down at that wig makers?'

'Yes, sir.'

'Are you likely to be much longer? I've just had an unpleasant phone call from Lord Tiverton at Tiverton Hall.'

Angel frowned.

'He's had a suit of armour stolen,' Harker continued. 'He's making a big meal of it. Get over there and see what you can do to settle him down. He's a big noise on the all-party Home Office ways and means committee. He can do us bit of good; I don't want him antagonized by some petty thieving, if you see what I mean.'

Angel knew exactly what he meant. His lordship was another friend of the chief constable and he thought that instructions had almost certainly come down from on high. 'I'll call in there on my way back.'

* * *

The sun was shining brightly, and Angel was standing outside the outbuildings of Tiverton Hall with his lordship, an elderly man incongruously dressed in brown tweed trousers, pyjama coat and slippers. He was bending forward leaning on a stick. His bald head was white and his face purple.

The two men were just inside the open door of one of the six outbuildings in a block, whose use had changed over the years from accommodating carriages and horses to garaging two modern cars, and storing dusty furnishings, pictures, rolled up marquees, loose tenting, garden furniture and tea chests full of china and assorted bric-a-brac. They were looking at a crude upright wooden structure, which was the means by which a suit of armour had been supported to display it in a standing position.

'You say it was there, my lord?' Angel said. 'You saw it, did you?'

'Of course I saw it. Dammit! It's been in the family for two hundred years. Seventy-three years to my own personal knowledge.'

Angel frowned. 'Why was it not in the house?'

Tiverton pulled a face. 'Her ladyship got fed up with it staring at her, she said, every time she came through the hall. So when we had the hall painted last year I had it moved here.'

'And when did you discover it was gone?'

'This morning. This very morning. I came back from Scotland yesterday, arrived at about six o'clock last night . . . I didn't go sniffing up and down the place then. I was damned bushed. Glad to get between the sheets. But I did have a look round this morning. Opened up everything. Good look round. You know. Somebody's got to do it. Larkin's all right, but he's not as conscientious as his predecessor, dear old Plimpton. Now Plimpton would have scouted round the place last night and spotted that it was missing in a trice.' He stopped and looked back at the house. He leaned over the stick, put a hand to his back and said, 'Now where the hell is he? I told him to meet us out here when you arrived.' His face contorted with pain.

Angel said, 'Do you want to sit down, my lord?'

'No. No. No. I want to get this matter dealt with then I can go back to bed. Where the hell is he?'

'Do you want me to go and find him?'

'No. You'd never find him. Wouldn't know where to look.'

Angel sighed. 'Well, how much was the suit of armour worth, my lord?'

'Irreplaceable. A million? Two million? I don't know. This wasn't a Victorian copy, you know. This was the real thing, about five or six hundred years old. Brought back from France by one of my ancestors. All the parts were there, Inspector . . . both gauntlets. It was made for a small man. My father thought it could have been the dauphin himself. I don't know.'

'I suppose it was insured?'

'What use is that? I couldn't buy another anything like that with the money it's insured for.'

Angel nodded. He expected the man was correct.

'Do you have a photograph of it?'

'Of course I have. I'll post one on to you. Shan't forget. You know, Angel, I have a good mind to sell up the whole bloody shebang and go and live in a bungalow at Filey or somewhere. If it wasn't for my son, that's what I would do. The responsibility and the bills would be far, far less. The relief of responsibility would be very welcome. And my wife and I would probably live longer. Just take Larkin and a maid for my dear wife. That jumped-up millionaire Chancey next door would buy the damned place in a flash. He's asked my solicitors twice about it. He's anxious to buy an acre of the bottom field for some vulgar commercial venture. Ha! Her ladyship won't hear of it. She still enjoys the pleasure of the lake, the motorboat and the fishing and so on.'

Angel stifled a smile. 'You have a lake, sir?'

'Behind those trees. Huge thing. We call it Lake Windermere. Nothing suits her ladyship better on a summer's

30

day than to be sat on the deck of the boat with paints and an easel, slapping out a Picasso or two. I wish they fetched half his money.'

A slight young man in a morning suit slipped quietly through the front door of the Hall and made his way down towards the coach houses.

Lord Tiverton saw him. 'Ah! Here he comes, Angel. At last. He'll be able to answer all your questions.'

Larkin seemed a pleasant enough young man, smartly dressed and brought up in the tradition of the profession, to be totally expressionless.

'Ah! There you are, Larkin. This is Inspector Angel . . . come about the suit of armour. Can you tell him when you last saw it . . . for certain, that is?'

'Yes, my lord. That would be about five o' clock on the day before we went to Scotland. That was Monday, the twenty-sixth of May. When I cleared the tea things off the lawn and brought the bamboo table back in here. It was certainly there then.'

Angel said, 'You are quite sure, Mr Larkin?'

'Absolutely, sir.'

'Hmm. Have you had any unusual characters around lately, calling at the door, making enquiries?'

Tiverton jumped in to answer, 'Can't think of any,' He glanced at the young man. 'Have we had anything like that, Larkin — gypsies or whatever.'

'I don't think so, my lord.'

'Who would know the suit of armour was here?' Angel asked, looking from one to the other.

It was Tiverton who replied. 'Anybody and everybody who visits us . . . in the summer, anyway. This door might well be left open if we were having tea in the garden with friends and acquaintances, which we frequently did when the weather was clement. But I can't think any of them would stoop so low.'

'Would they know its value?'

'Would hardly have thought so,' his lordship said thoughtfully, then added, 'No. I think not.'

'Who knew you were away?' Angel said.

'Loads of people . . . tradespeople . . . all the staff and their families . . . my doctor . . . the bridge club . . . but you can't suspect them, Inspector. Dammit, some of them are my friends. They are the cream of the town. Anyway, the house is entirely alarmed. The system, I am reliably informed, is foolproof.'

'Unfortunately, it didn't include these outbuildings,' Angel said.

'No,' Tiverton grunted, then angrily muttered something unintelligible, turned and began to stagger back towards the front door of the Hall. Larkin quickly joined him.

'I'd like to take a look around the grounds if I may?' Angel called.

Tiverton stopped, looked back and impatiently said, 'You can poke around out here for as long as you like, if it will help to bring back that armour, Inspector. But I must return to bed.'

'Right, my lord.'

'Take Larkin. He may be of service to you.'

The man in the morning suit arched an eyebrow briefly, then remembered himself, nodded dutifully towards Tiverton, turned and rejoined Angel at the door of the garage.

Angel rubbed his chin.

Lord Tiverton, in spite of the pain, soon reached the front door of the house and went inside.

After a moment, Angel turned to the young man and said, 'Have you any idea how this suit of armour might have been stolen?'

'Not really,' Larkin said. 'It was quite heavy and awkward. It wouldn't have been easy for one man to carry away. It was in about six pieces, you see.' He spoke in a more normal and relaxed voice out of the presence of his lordship.

'Yes. And how was the garage broken into?' Angel asked, turning round and looking for the lock.

'It wasn't locked, Inspector. It's never been locked. None of the garages is locked. It's not a problem. Well, it's never been seen to be a problem until now. Strangers or unsavoury people do not frequent this area and certainly not as far down Creesforth Drive as this. We are well off the beaten track. Even the post is delivered by van. We are aware that the occasional person walks their dog on the old path between the grounds and the farmer's field on the west side, but there's an eight-foot wall most of the way down. And the neighbours on the east side are the Chanceys, a very respectable family. They have that big modern house with the swimming pool and the tennis court. Frank Chancey owns that big chain of timber merchants and DIY places. You must have heard of Chancey's Timber Merchants? Branches all over the place.'

Angel raised his head. Of course he recalled the name, the signs and the persistent, annoying and repetitive advertisements on television. He made a mental note of where the rich man lived.

'Where is the lake, Mr Larkin?'

'It is just beyond the trees,' he said pointing behind the garages. 'I'll show you. This way.' He began striding out on the gravel down a path that led through a curtain of trees and bushes to a pleasing sight beyond them of a small blue lake with a grey carved stone pillared bridge, decorated with potted flowers across it, and a small motorboat moored to a short wooden quay. They stood there a few moments. Angel was taking in the view. He was quietly surprised that such a delightful outlook could be hidden in the backwoods of Bromersley.

They walked down to the little quay and the motorboat. It was rocking slightly in the warm, south-west wind.

'Do the Tivertons spend much time out here in the good weather?'

'She does. She likes to potter in the garden sometimes and she enjoys painting . . . all he does out of doors is tootle round the lake in the boat, amusing their grandchildren.'

Suddenly there was the ringing of a mobile phone.

Larkin realized it was his. 'Excuse me,' he said. He opened the phone and spoke into it. 'Yes, my lord.'

Angel could hear a few distorted words, then the conversation seemed to end abruptly.

Larkin turned to Angel as he pocketed the mobile. 'I have to go. His lordship wants his hot-water bottle refilling. Is there anything more I can assist you with, Inspector?'

Angel smiled appreciatively. 'No, thank you, Mr Larkin. I will quickly take a look at one or two things out here, and then I'll be on my way. Please tell his lordship that I will do all I can to catch the thief.'

'Right, sir,' Larkin said, then he dashed away.

When the noise of Larkin's footsteps on the gravel had faded away Angel looked down at the bulrushes close to where he was standing, then across the length of the rippling blue water to the green bushes and trees at the other side. Thousands of reflections of the sun danced gently on the water. He rubbed his chin thoughtfully . . . we live in an age when if something looks easy to steal — regardless of its value — people will steal it. Ballpoint pens in some banks are fastened to the desk by a chain. Multiple grocery chains put some small, expensive items in security boxes. In this situation, a suit of armour worth millions had been stolen. He could imagine that it would be great to help dress a theatre or a film set, but it could not be offered for sale for that purpose. This particular one would presumably have been immediately spotted. How then would a thief dispose of it? How would he convert the suit of armour into hard cash? Perceptive antique dealers and leading auctioneers wouldn't want to handle it without knowing the source. Was it possible a loyal citizen from, say France, might seek to wish to have the armour returned to its native country? Like the Greeks with the Elgin marbles. There are very wealthy people who have stolen hordes of paintings and sculptures which are too well known to be shown publicly, who may have widened their interest to include antiquities. He rubbed his chin.

FOUR

Angel returned to his office and glanced at the pile of post on his desk. He wrinkled his nose. It hardly ever seemed to get any less. He fingered thoughtfully through the envelopes, but it was pointless: his mind was on the wig maker. He wondered why anyone would want to murder him. He began in his thoughts to go systematically through the list of possible motives. He was interrupted by a knock at the door.

'Come in.'

It was DS Trevor Crisp, a handsome, well-dressed young man much admired by the ladies. It was rumoured that he had a relationship with the best looking unattached young woman in the station, WPC Leisha Baverstock, but his love life was neither straightforward nor comprehensible.

'You wanted me, sir?'

Angel's eyes flashed. His jaw tightened.

'I wanted you two hours ago, at a murder scene,' he snapped. 'A wig maker, Peter Wolff of Market Street, was shot dead in the early hours. That's when I wanted you. And then at Lord Tiverton's place, a suit of armour worth millions was stolen. I could have done with you there as well.'

Crisp looked sheepish. 'I heard about the wig maker, sir, but I was tied up with a house burglary; thieves got away with the contents of a deep freezer in a garage. It wasn't a major incident, but I couldn't just *dump* the woman.'

Angel's face was red. He blinked. He couldn't resist saying, 'I don't know, lad? You've dumped plenty of women in the past!'

Crisp's eyes opened wide. He was thinking what to reply. He wasn't usually stuck for words.

Angel moved on quickly. 'This wig maker, Peter Wolff, did you know him?'

'No, sir. Heard of him. I reckon there isn't a woman in the town who hasn't. Some of them would've given their eye teeth to have had a wig made by him. He knew the hair business backwards. You know, he knew what constituted a glamorous hairdo. Expensive though, I think.'

'Yes, but what was he like as a man?'

'Don't know, sir.'

'I want you to ask around. Find out where he went. What made him tick. What his interests were. Who his friends were. Who his enemies were. I've had a cursory look over his shop and flat but learned very little. Surely there's more to life than eating and sleeping and making wigs? There is no apparent reason for his murder. There's got to be a motive.'

Crisp looked at him thoughtfully.

'I've got Ron Gawber asking around Market Street, where his shop is. His neighbours and so on. I want you to start asking in women's hairdressers. They are his natural competitors, I suppose. Might be up for a bit of gossip. But don't waste time, lad. Work is piling up.'

'Right, sir.'

After Crisp had closed the door Angel picked up the phone and tapped in the CID office number.

It was soon answered by Probationer PC Ahmed Ahaz, aged twenty. He was a handsome, shy, very intelligent and enthusiastic young man who came third at Aykley Heads police college in Durham and had been on Angel's team since joining the force as a humble cadet three years previously.

'Yes, sir?' he said brightly.

'Ahmed, there's a man, Peter Wolff, wig maker . . . find out if he has any form. Also, there's a man called Larkin, check him out while you're at it. I haven't got his Christian name. And bring me a cup of tea.'

'Right, sir.'

He replaced the phone.

There was a knock at the door. It was Gawber.

'Ah, Ron. What have you got?'

'Can't find anything much on Wolff, sir. He seems to have been a quiet sort of bird. Kept himself to himself. Pleasant. Courteous. Paid his way. Bought sandwiches most every day from the shop next door. Lived on his own. Some of the shop-keepers didn't know he lived over the shop and were surprised when I told them. The card shop lady opposite thought he must be well off. She'd only seen well-heeled people go into his shop. It was appointment only. The door was always locked. Callers had to press a button to get into the place.'

'Did she recognize any of his callers?'

'No, sir. Only that they were . . . well dressed. No riff-raff, she said.'

Angel frowned. 'He was only a wig maker, dammit. Why keep the door locked? What had he got in there, the crown jewels?'

'Maybe he was just being selective . . . keeping a high standard.'

Angel rubbed his chin. 'Hmmm. Come to think of it, there was no intruder alarm system in the building.'

Gawber nodded. 'That's right. Maybe SOCO will come across a safe?'

'Aye. What about his next of kin?'

'Nothing known about that, sir.'

'Right. Well, find out his bank and let's look at his finances. His doctor, chase that up and anything else about him.'

The phone rang. He reached out for it. It was Superintendent Harker.

'Come along up here, right away, lad,' he said. There was an unpleasant click in his ear and the line went dead.

Angel's face dropped. He replaced the phone and turned to Gawber. 'The super wants me. Can't think what for. There's a cup of tea coming. You have it. If I'm going to be long, I'll give you a buzz. All right?'

Gawber nodded.

Angel dashed up the corridor to Harker's office.

'Come in, Angel,' Harker said. 'Got something special on.'

Angel lifted his head. Sounded interesting. Or was it something with a catch to it? It would be just like Harker to dress something dodgy up by saying it was 'something special'.

'You've heard of Chancey's DIY and timber importers?' Harker said importantly.

Angel nodded.

'Well, Frank Chancey, multi-millionaire and boss of that outfit, is on a sort of nodding acquaintance with the chief constable. Same club, charity boards and so on. He's in a spot of trouble. Just rung up the chief, and the chief has just phoned me. His wife Katrina has disappeared. She's a model, and her agent's reported her missing to her husband first thing this morning. Possibly run off. Wants us to find her.'

Angel's eyes flashed. He wasn't pleased. 'A misper, sir? That's a job for the Salvation Army, isn't it?'

Harker sniffed, then said, 'Not in this case.'

'You know that at present I'm up to my neck looking for the murderer of a wig maker, sir. Or is looking for this millionaire's runaway wife more important than looking for a killer? She's probably run off with the chauffeur or the milkman or somebody, for a change of pace.'

'Don't get smart, lad. The chief constable is still my boss and I'm still yours. And you know that the chief wouldn't be pushing an order through without good reason, and he's not obliged to tell you or me everything he knows. Now he wants it looking into by us, and that's as much as you need to know.'

Angel felt properly put in his place. He nodded and said, 'Right, sir. I'll fit it in the best way I can.'

'There's an appointment been made for you for nine o' clock tomorrow morning, at Frank Chancey's home.'

'I might have to be somewhere else,' he said, just to be awkward.

'Cancel it!' Harker snapped. 'You'll need his address.'

'I've got it, sir.'

He went out and closed the door.

* * *

It was 8.58 a.m. on Tuesday, 1 July.

Angel had put on his best suit and new shoes; he was going to see Frank Chancey, multi-millionaire and allegedly a big number in the town. He drove the BMW along Creesforth

Road, turned down into Creesforth Drive, a narrow private road. He passed Tiverton Hall on the left, then travelled alongside a red brick wall for 250 yards until it curved into a short entrance. The words 'Chancey House' were fashioned out of wrought iron and cemented into the wall. He turned the wheel and saw a pair of black wrought iron gates, which were wide open. He drove between the stone gateposts but had to stop abruptly as a big yellow bulldozer reversed across his path in front of him. The driver, a young man, shirtless and wearing a hard hat waved his thanks, then stopped, lowered the dozer blade and began to push forward a mound of soil. He seemed to be in the process of building some sort of an embankment. As soon as the bulldozer had moved out of the way Angel let in the clutch and followed the drive between several strategically placed conifers and clusters of evergreen bushes located to make for privacy, round to the front of the house.

The drive opened up into a large square area of silver-grey gravel directly in front of the main house entrance. In the middle of the square a circular hole about twenty feet in diameter had been excavated, and two men in hard hats were leaning on large shovels watching a ready-mix vehicle discharge its heavy load into the cavity. There were two other ready-mix wagons behind them, their cylinders noisily revolving, apparently awaiting their turn to unload.

Angel wondered why so much was happening when the lady of the house was apparently missing. He drove around the workmen towards the front entrance and stopped. He got out of the car and locked it. He walked briskly across the gravel to the front door, climbed up the four steps and found the bell push. It was promptly answered by a smartly dressed young man in a morning suit. His accent showed he was from the Dublin area.

'Yes, sir? You'd be the police inspector?' he said with a smile.

'Detective Inspector Angel, to see Mr Chancey.'

'Yes, sir. Please come in. Mr Chancey is expecting you. Please follow me.'

The house was magnificent. He was glad he'd put on his best suit. It looked as if Chancey had bought a piece of Buckingham Palace and had it towed up to Bromersley. He strode out on the plush carpet behind the smart young man. He could smell fresh paint. He looked round. Why could he smell fresh paint?

'My name is Lyle, sir. Is there anything I can do for you before you go in to see Mr Chancey?'

. Angel frowned. It was probably his euphemistic way of enquiring if he needed directions to the bathroom.

'No thank you, Mr Lyle.'

They marched down a corridor, passing a dozen or more big oil paintings on the walls, of ugly, bald men, possibly Chancey's ancestors, until they reached double doors at the end.

'Here we are,' Lyle said. He knocked loudly on one door, opened it, put his head in and said, 'Inspector Angel, boss.'

'Right, Jimmy,' he heard a man's voice call out.

Lyle opened the other door, ushered Angel in and closed the doors behind him.

It was a big room, furnished like the sitting-room of a four-star hotel, with one major difference: in the middle of it was a desk as big as a bed.

A smart, tall, handsome man of about thirty-four or thirty-five stood up behind the desk, hand outstretched. 'Come in, Inspector. Chancey is the name, Frank Chancey. Thank you for coming. Please take a seat. May I say that you come highly recommended.'

Angel wondered who by. His eyes flitted up and down the man, taking stock. Chancey had all the characteristics of the moneyed classes: hand sewn dark suit cut as sharp as a heroin needle, silk shirt, diamond cuff-links, Roché watch, gold signet ring, skin tanned that distinctive apricot by the Caribbean sun, and a mop of jet-black curly hair going distinguished white at the temples.

At the same time Chancey had been looking Angel up and down. He seemed to approve. He indicated a chair opposite the desk and Angel took it.

'I expect your . . . chief constable has told you about my wife, Inspector?'

'Only that she has disappeared, sir. Perhaps you'd like to tell me all about it?'

'Yes, of course.' Chancey rubbed his chin. 'Where to start?' he said and licked his bottom lip. 'It's hard to try to convey five years of my life into a few minutes, but, well it all started with a row. Nothing serious, you understand. But a row. We didn't often have a disagreement, but that's what happened. Families have them all the time, don't they?'

Angel hesitated. He didn't want to agree, but he had to concede it happened. He pursed his lips and rocked his head a couple of times.

'Katrina and I normally get on very well, *very well indeed*. But, anyway, it was one of those days. So to try to stop the arguing, I said that she should have a holiday. That she *needed* a holiday. It was a way of bribing her, I admit it. I said she should go somewhere nice, somewhere . . . where she could relax. I should explain, Inspector, that my wife is a model. Quite well-known out there . . . and on both sides of the Atlantic. You may have heard of her. She uses the professional name of Katrina?'

43

Angel mentally scoured his memory. He couldn't place the name, but then again he easily admitted to having little or no knowledge of prevailing culture. He had an all-encompassing word for it: it sounded like scrap, but it only had four letters.

'I'm afraid not, sir.'

Undeterred, Chancey continued. 'I gave her a handsome cheque, reserved a suite for her at the Hotel Leonardo Quincento in Rome. It was the most expensive place I could think of. I booked a plane ticket to Rome and organized transport to the airport. I thought I had dealt with the situation pretty well. I thought she would fly off, enjoy herself, buy a few clothes, relax, and return in a couple of weeks in a happy, settled mood and life would go on.'

Angel looked round the room. He took in the framed photographs on the walls. They were all of the same young woman. Strikingly beautiful, long legs, big bosom, deep cleavage, blue eyes, full lips, long blonde hair. He assumed it was Katrina. Some of the photographs displayed more than Angel would have liked to be shown of *his* wife to all and sundry.

'These photographs,' he said at length. 'Are they all of your wife?'

'Yes, indeed,' Chancey said, smiling. He breathed in noisily, stuck out his chest, glanced round at them and added, 'Aren't they . . . *sensational?*'

Angel rubbed his chin. Sensational might be the word Chancey wanted to use. The word Angel would have used would have been simply . . . mucky.

'Yes,' he managed to say, but his lack of enthusiasm might have been obvious. He moved quickly on. 'Then what happened, sir?'

Chancey peered thoughtfully across the desk. He had lost the thread. His eyes moved to left and then to right. He picked it up after a few seconds. 'I got a phone call from her agent in London. The model agency. She had seemingly not turned up for a shoot. Now in the modelling business, Inspector, a missed appointment is almost as criminal as assassinating the pope. She would never have forgotten or overlooked a modelling appointment, especially a shoot. She was modelling mad; it was her life!'

Angel appreciated the point.

'What was the name of the agency, sir? And who spoke to you?' Angel said.

'The agency's called "Top Notch" and the woman who phoned me was called Melanie something or other.'

Angel nodded smiled and with a gesture invited Chancey to continue.

'So when the agency phoned me and told me she was not answering her mobile and that she hadn't been in touch with them for some weeks, I naturally became concerned. I immediately phoned the hotel in Rome, discovered she had not booked in and that the suite had not been occupied for the last fourteen days, also the airline had by this time sent the unclaimed ticket with the bill to my office address and yesterday morning it had filtered its way to me. I got Jimmy to check on her car, and it was here, parked up in the garage. I have no idea where she is.'

'Can we sort these dates out, sir? When did you book the hotel and so on? When should she have gone, and when did her agency phone you?'

'Friday, the thirteenth, we had the row. That was also the same day that I booked the hotel, the airplane and a car. All by phone. The arrangements were made for early the next day, the fourteenth, of course. The agency phoned yesterday morning to say they hadn't heard from her.'

'So it's clear that your wife didn't go to Rome then, sir. Is it reasonable to think that these past two weeks she stayed in this country?'

He hesitated. 'I think it is, Inspector.'

'Hmm. Have you any children?'

'No.'

'Have either of you been married before?'

'No.'

'Very well. Is there some particular place, relative, friend, lover, whatever, where you consider she might be or has been these past two weeks?'

Chancey's mouth tightened. 'No.'

'It would be a big job to trace every friend, relative or acquaintance of your wife, people she may have struck up a relationship with in her lifetime. And believe me, Mr Chancey, we do that, most thoroughly, but it's time consuming. And we would only undertake such an action if there were some fact to indicate that a crime has been committed. Ten thousand people go missing in this country every year: over three thousand are never traced. I have to ask you, have you any such evidence?'

'Not specifically,' Chancey said quietly. 'I have told you all I know.' His hand went to his face. He rubbed his hand across his chin. He spoke quietly, confidently. 'No. But I'm nevertheless getting very worried, Inspector. Very worried. She has been missing for two weeks. We did not part on the best of terms. Something has happened to her.'

'You may have to face up to the possibility, Mr Chancey, that Katrina . . . may have left you of her own free will.'

'I have already considered that and dismissed it, because if she had, Inspector, I tell you she would still have kept her appointment at the shoot, wherever it was, chatted on her mobile phone, she couldn't keep off the damned thing, and used her credit cards. But she hasn't done any of those things.'

Angel raised his head. These facts, if that was what they were, were greatly significant, but not conclusive. Many women, particularly those of independent means, could and have told their overbearing husbands where to stick their money.

'You'd better give me her mobile, credit card numbers and bank details. It won't take long to do a check on them.'

Chancey broke off, opened desk drawers, consulted address book and bank statement folder and supplied Angel with numbers which he wrote on the back of an envelope taken from his inside pocket. He then considered carefully his next question.

'Are *you* suggesting that she has been abducted, sir?'

'I don't know.'

'Or murdered?'

Chancey's face tightened. He looked shocked. He swallowed and said, 'I don't know.' He stood up, turned away from the desk and walked over to the window.

Angel rubbed his chin as he watched the handsome, athletic figure standing framed in the window, his back to him. He was looking out at a long lawn and then the foothills of the Pennines. He saw him fumbling with a handkerchief. After a few moments he seemed to end whatever he was doing with it. He stuffed it in his top pocket, turned back to face the policeman and said, 'Inspector Angel, I think we have danced around the disappearance of my wife for long enough. You must institute a search for Katrina or I will.'

'I need something to indicate foul play, sir. We don't know why she didn't go to that hotel in Rome. Maybe she simply didn't want to go there. Was it you who suggested that particular hotel?'

'Yes, as a matter of fact it was, but she has stayed there before. She loves it there. She's mad about Rome. We stayed there together for a few days last year. She adored it.'

'We have to assume there is no foul play unless there is something to suggest the contrary. I assume that there has been no communication directly from her since she went, nor have you had a ransom note or a phone call about her since?'

'Not yet.'

Angel's eyebrows went up. Seemed he was expecting one.

'I'll speak to my super, sir. If he believes a search should be made, then that's what we'll do.'

Chancey slumped down in the chair. 'Very well,' he said. 'I'll hold back for two more days. If the police cannot help and there is no change or news, I will instigate my own private team and begin an independent search.'

Angel frowned. He hoped he wouldn't do that. Crime solving these days was a highly professional job. He wouldn't enjoy tripping up over amateurs.

'Very well, sir,' he said. 'I don't think we can take this any further. I'll get back to you very soon.'

He stood up to leave.

Chancey rose, pressed a button, then came round the side of the desk and up to him.

'Thank you, Inspector Angel. It has been really good meeting you. I like you, and you are a really tough negotiator. I like that in a man.'

Angel enjoyed the words, but he didn't believe them for one moment.

'Thank you, sir,' Angel said. 'One more question I would like to ask. Idle curiosity, nothing more. What is all the activity outside? I was nearly swept away by a bulldozer as I came in your front gate.'

'I am sorry about that,' Chancey said. 'I am making lots of changes to the homestead for when Katrina returns. The bulldozer is building a banking that will support a short pathway. On the top of it, I am going to have a sheltered walkway built that will lead to a gazebo. It will be sited at the highest point of my land, and give us a magnificent view of the countryside to the south-west whilst being sheltered from the rain. In addition, we had been talking about building a marble fountain at the front of the house. She thought it would be a fabulous improvement to its appearance and could also be soothing. I must say, I agreed with her. So I am pressing on with building of it in her absence. The stonemasons are flying in from Capri tomorrow. It will be a terrific surprise for her when she comes back. It's costing a pretty penny, best part of eighty thousand pounds, but she's worth it.'

Angel nodded. And then, he suddenly thought of the unpaid gas bill. He was still about £60 short.

FIVE

The sun beat down on the Tarmac surface causing shimmering waves of hot air to rise on the road ahead. The bus turned off the A61 road north of Harrogate and rocked its way along a leafy unmade country lane, shaking its payload of twenty-four ladies, aged from forty to eighty-two years of age, all members of the Bromersley Women's Guild. They were off on their regular Tuesday afternoon excursion, and this was the long-planned trip to Seymour Timms's famous chrysanthemum garden.

Terry Shaw, their regular driver, addressed the ladies through the driver's microphone.

'Sorry about the bumps, ladies. Please keep in your seats until we get there. It's the only road in and out of the place. Seymour Timms's garden is in the middle of nowhere. But we'll be there in a couple of ticks.'

The ladies seemed pleased, even excited at the prospect of seeing and meeting the famous man. They remembered his many appearances on the television and radio on Gardener's

Question Time, Chelsea Flower Show and the like in the eighties and nineties, and they wondered how the years had treated him.

Mary Angel was on the front seat with another lady from the church. They held tightly on to the chromium tubing round the top of the stairwell throughout the bumpy journey down the country lane. Eventually the bus stopped as it reached a big double gate that was falling to pieces. Beside it there was a scruffy old man in boots, corduroy trousers, a short-sleeved shirt and a yellow boater. He had a pipe in his mouth but it didn't seem to be lit. He had opened one part of the gate and dragged an oil drum in front it to stop it swinging to, and was now struggling to push open the other. He had suspended his walking stick on a rail on the gate while he lifted and heaved the old gate open wide enough to admit the bus.

Mary stared through the window at the scene and at the patched-up fencing at each side of the gates. Looking beyond she could see a large old grey house looking very sad and in need of attention, repair and paint. She exchanged glances with the lady in the next seat. They both looked dismayed. There were sounds of disappointment and comment at the dowdiness of the place from some of the other ladies behind them.

At a wave from the old man, Terry Shaw let in the clutch and the bus moved forward through the gates on to a short track towards the ramshackle house, then it turned sharp right and went along for about a hundred yards, eventually stopping on a hard earthy patch.

Through the front window of the bus could be seen the most magnificent show of flowers — all chrysanthemums — planted in long rows of various colours like a Fair Isle pullover almost as far as the eye could see. The ladies were overjoyed.

51

This was a great surprise. Their faces changed and their eyes glowed in anticipation. They gasped, laughed and chatted excitedly. Some began to get to their feet.

Through the mike Terry Shaw said, 'Now then, ladies, isn't that a wonderful sight?'

There were various excited cries of 'What a surprise! Magnificent! What colours! Wonderful!'

Terry smiled. 'Will you please keep your seats, ladies? Mr Timms himself will be along directly to speak to you.'

They looked about everywhere for the great man, but there was no sign of life anywhere. Behind them next to the house were six huge greenhouses. Some had glass panes broken and seemed to be standing at unsafe angles; all needed a good coat of paint. They turned back and enjoyed looking at the many rows of colours and marvelled at how regular the formation was and were wondering if there were any plants to buy or mementoes to take back. Some needed the loo and others wanted a cup of tea. Suddenly, they heard the bus door slide open and up the steps came the same old man who had struggled to open the gates for them. He smiled and nodded at Terry, who reciprocated, unhooked the microphone from its holder and passed it over to him.

The old man took the unlit pipe out of his mouth, smiled and said, 'Thank you, Terry.'

Then he looked down the bus at the cheerful, curious faces and said, 'And good afternoon, everybody. I am Seymour Timms. And thank you for coming to see my garden.'

He had a warm, friendly, confident speaking voice and smiled frequently throughout, waving the pipe around now and again for emphasis. Although old and angular with a thin sad face, the ladies were fascinated by him and listened attentively to every word.

'Now, some of you may remember me from years gone by?'

There were some calls of, 'Yes' and at least one lady clapped her hands.

He smiled, showing his teeth; one was missing to the side of his jaw. He must have seen more than eighty summers.

'You are very kind. Well, all that is behind me now. As I have grown older, I hope I have also grown wiser. And instead of being a gardening jack of all trades, I have specialized in the growing of one particular species. I have retired completely from the uncertain world of TV and radio, seeming to mesmerize audiences with clever answers to routine questions, for the more sober life of cultivating chrysanthemums up here in the backwoods. For twenty years now, I have done very little else. That's why today in my garden you can see over seventy-two varieties of the humble chrysanthemum in innumerable colours and colour permutations, from bonsai to large exhibition varieties, also incurved, reflexed, pompons, spiders, quills spoons and so on. And I am still going on . . . until every variety can be propagated in every colour. It has become my lifetime ambition. To achieve it, I have had to make sacrifices. The greenhouses are not in the best of condition and it is not safe enough for you to go anywhere near them. The house needs fixing here and there. It is comfortable enough for an old man who lives on his own, but it is not smart enough to entertain elegant ladies. So those two areas, I fear, must be out of bounds. And the fences and gates also need renewing. I hope to attend to all these things in due course, but at the moment I simply haven't the time. I have no staff. Everything that is done here in my garden and in my house I have to do myself. Nobody will come out here and work alongside me, the way I would like, so I am resigned to attending to everything myself. I don't mind this. I am not complaining, just explaining why things are as they are.'

He paused a moment, sucked on the unlit pipe, pulled it out again and continued, 'Now that I have explained all that, I am very pleased to welcome you into my garden, and, of course, there is absolutely no charge. Now, if you wish to buy any plants, there are only chrysanthemums, I'm afraid. Everything in the nearest two rows can go, but positively no others. Please help yourselves and put your money in the blue and white dish in the conservatory. I am sorry, I have no time to be a shop-keeper. You may use my loo free of charge. It is through the door at the side of the conservatory. Please leave it clean and tidy. I regret that there are no facilities for making cups of tea or sandwiches or any catering, but no doubt Terry will take you on to Betty's café in Harrogate, if time in your programme allows it. I close the gates at four o'clock prompt. So please be out by then. And please be kind enough not to make me any work. If you drop anything, move anything or break anything there is only one person to pick it up, put it back or repair it, and that's me. I hope to use the limited energy and time I have left into generating new varieties and colours of chrysanthemums. I am an old man and frankly, come five o'clock I can work no more, my energy is spent. Lastly, I hope you will receive great pleasure from looking round my garden. Feel free to enjoy the flowers, the colour and the fragrance. Now I must leave you. I have some forty rows to hoe by Friday. Lovely to meet you all, and I hope you will come back again sometime. Thank you for your patient attention. Good afternoon.'

He raised his hat to show an almost bald head, replaced it, put the pipe in his mouth, handed the mike back to Terry, recovered his stick and stepped down the bus steps and out into the sunshine.

The ladies muttered excitedly to each other.

'Please be back here by half past three,' Terry said into the mike. 'If we get away promptly we will have time to call at Betty's for a quick cup of tea. Half past three then, ladies. Thank you.'

The ladies bustled off the bus and swarmed down the path to see the many different types of blooms at close range.

Mary Angel rushed up the path to the furthest point of the garden and worked her way back. All the visitors gawped in wonderment at the differently shaped petals and the amazing range of colours and combinations of colours. There were not many plants to buy and the rare varieties were not among them, but Mary chose a nice pink one in a pot and then crossed to the big house to the conservatory to find the blue-and-white dish in which to leave her money.

The conservatory was crowded out with flowers; every possible space and ledge was occupied with chrysanthemums in pots on boxes, window ledges, the floor, even on a rickety table partly covered with earth which had spilled out of the pots and never been cleared up. Mary found the blue-and-white dish easily enough; it was on the congested table. She recognized it to be a beautiful old Wedgwood fruit bowl, which she thought must be quite valuable. She noted that there must be about a hundred pounds in notes and coins in the dish as she dropped her money into it to pay for her plant. As she did so, she observed that the edge of the earth-covered table was scalloped in a particular way. She took a coin out of her purse and gently scraped some of the soil off the table-top. As she did do, her heart beat increased. She then kneeled down and looked underneath it. Her pulse began to race even faster. She sighed loudly, though, when she saw that the table was propped up at one corner by a pile of old, thick books.

A leg had been removed or broken off, leaving the four-legged table with only three legs. She stood up and shook her head. She saw what she felt was a calamity, a disaster, because she instinctively knew that that table had been made by none other than master craftsman, Thomas Chippendale!

She ran out of the conservatory and up to the bus to see if she could see Seymour Timms. She looked in every direction, but he was not to be seen. Then she spotted him a long way away in the middle of a row of flowers, his hat pulled well down on his head for protection from the sun, pipe in mouth and hoe in hand pushing and pulling weeds from between the plants. She ran up the path and carefully picked her way through the row towards him.

'Mr Timms,' she called.

He didn't seem to hear her first call. His mind was concentrating on the job in hand, his brown, bony arms and elbows pushing and pulling the hoe backwards and forwards deftly through the soil.

'Mr Timms,' she repeated, almost upon him.

He looked up. 'Oh.' He wasn't pleased, but he doffed his hat and said, 'You wanted me, dear lady?'

Mary flashed her best smile, which melted him briefly.

'How can I be of service?'

'Mr Timms, I am sorry to disturb you. I have bought a plant and put the money in the dish in the conservatory as you requested.'

'I am very grateful, I am sure,' he said, but he didn't mean it, and Mary knew it.

'Did you know the dish is an old Wedgwood fruit bowl, which must be quite valuable?' she said.

'Yes, I believe it is. It does the job admirably though, don't you think? I do not use a fruit bowl myself. I leave any fruit that I have in its bag until I want to eat it. Saves time and washing up.'

Mary was struck momentarily dumb.

'Now, if you'll excuse me, I must get on,' he said looking down at the soil and pushing away at the hoe.

'The table it is on is Chippendale,' she blurted out. 'Thomas Chippendale, I believe.'

'Really?'

'It has a leg missing.'

'Really?'

'Do you know where the missing leg is, Mr Timms?'

'No. I don't think I do. Does it matter? It does its job admirably well, don't you think?'

'It would be worth a lot of money if you knew where the other leg was.'

'Well, thank you very much for that information. Now, if you would excuse me, I want to finish this row before five o'clock.'

'Oh. Yes,' she stammered. 'The thing is, I would like to buy the table.'

'Oh dear,' he said wearily. 'That's not possible, I am afraid, dear lady. The table is not for sale.'

'I think you know where the missing leg is, don't you?'

'Well . . . erm, I might do, but what is the point? I really could not be bothered with it, dear lady. Besides, the table is not for sale.'

'If the leg was put back on the table, Mr Timms, it could be a very beautiful piece of furniture.'

'I daresay, but I am a horticulturist, not a carpenter.'

'But by neglect, you are throwing away history. Chippendale furniture is extremely rare. It should be nurtured. It's your and my heritage. It's a legacy handed down by our fathers. Antiques are being slowly wasted away, Mr Timms. They are too valuable to be neglected. Everybody should have at least one antique piece in their house.'

'Oh dear.' He sighed. 'Maybe you are right.'

She thought he was weakening.

'Could you tell me where the missing leg is, Mr Timms?'

He shook his head. He wasn't pleased. 'I think it is being used to support the doorpost of my main greenhouse. Now perhaps you would permit me to press on with my work?'

'Will you show it to me?'

'What for?'

She looked into his eyes and gave him her best smile. '*Please*,' she said drawing the word out persuasively.

He rubbed his chin, pulled a face with the corners of his mouth turned down. 'Oh. Very well,' he said resignedly and stabbed the hoe in the ground. 'Come with me, dear lady. Very quickly then. You will see that it cannot possibly be moved.'

Seymour Timms strode boldly off the growing area. Mary Angel turned round and picked her way carefully between the rows of plants back to the path. She followed him to the rather overgrown area of the greenhouses. The edges of the pathways to the doorways were covered in nettles and dandelions. The biggest greenhouse was huge and as they approached even Mary could see that the uprights were not vertical and that it was not a safe area to be. It was just as Timms had said. It was decidedly precarious. The door was open and held there by a brick. He pointed down to the face side of a shapely piece of wood sunk in the earth and wedged tightly between the two doorjambs.

'There is the leg,' he said. 'With that leg wedged in there, I can now open and close the door,' he said proudly and gave her a demonstration. 'There you are. I couldn't do that before. So you see, it could not possibly be removed. It could unsettle the structure of the greenhouse and the whole thing could come shattering down on to all my plants and seedlings.'

Mary's face dropped. She realized that what he said might well be true.

'Now, my dear lady, you see that the table could not possibly be repaired and is therefore not for sale.'

Her face dropped.

'I hope that you see that,' he continued. 'Now, if you will excuse me, I must return to my hoeing.'

He looked down at her and awaited her response.

Mary Angel was thinking. The wheels and cogs whizzed round at great speed. At length she said, 'Very well, Mr Timms, I will buy the table from you with just the three legs.'

He smiled. 'Ha. And what would you do with a table with only three legs? No. No. No,' he said and laughed as he walked away.

'Two hundred pounds, Mr Timms,' she called.

He stopped, turned, and still smiling, said, 'No. No. No. Dear lady. The table as it is is more useful to me doing the job it does, even if it is Chippendale.'

'I am *certain* it is Chippendale, Mr Timms.'

'Well, so be it. It is probably full of woodworm and beyond restoration. I'm sorry. Now I must get on.'

'Three hundred pounds,' Mary said boldly.

He wrinkled his nose. 'You really are most persistent. Please put your money away, dear lady. Chippendale or not, in that condition it is worth far more to me as a humble pot stand than to you as an antique table. I would not dream of taking your money under false pretences. And frankly, I am not at all certain it is Chippendale.'

'Five hundred pounds, Mr Timms,' she said determinedly. 'I can't afford any more.'

Timms's face creased with dismay. 'Do you not see, dear lady, my predicament. I do not want the money. If I could buy time with it, maybe I would, but alas I can't. I cannot be bothered to find some other table to fit all those pots back in there. I am tired, weary. I am not a do-it-yourself-er. For me, it would just be more work for me, changing things around. I cannot do with change. Change is the bugbear of my life.'

'Mr Timms, I am very keen to have that table. Do you not see that with a bit of planning, you could get a joiner in to build you some really sensible shelving. With a bit of careful thought you could get a lot more pots in that conservatory if it were planned out and shelving put exactly where you want it. Now a joiner could do that for you in no time at all and it wouldn't cost you five hundred pounds.'

He blinked and cocked his head to one side.

SIX

'How much?' he bawled. 'Five hundred pounds?'

'Don't shout,' she said. 'You're always *shouting*.'

'But five hundred pounds . . . I mean. For a table to put a telephone on. It's ridiculous!'

'It's an antique. It's an investment. In years to come it will be worth thousands. And it'll make the hall look really smart.'

'That means there's only a hundred and six pounds of that windfall left towards the gas bill.'

'That's not going towards the gas bill! And it's not a windfall. It's a legacy. And I've got plans for that hundred and six pounds.'

Angel ran his hand through his hair.

'Plans. What plans?'

'That hundred and six pounds is needed for something important.'

'For goodness' sake, Mary. What's the use of a hall table when we have a gas bill to pay? And what's the something that's important?'

'It needs a bit of restoration?'

His jaw almost dropped to the floor. 'What does? Your little Chippendale table costing five hundred pounds needs a hundred and six pounds worth of restoration?'

Mary turned round from the sink. She put her hands on her hips. 'Look here, Michael Angel. That money was left to *me* by a relation of *mine*, an uncle.'

'A great-uncle.'

'And I want to buy something useful to remember him by.'

'You've never even seen him.'

'That's nothing to do with it. It's a legacy! And it is not going to go into the communal housekeeping pot. The table is paid for. I've given him a cheque. The deal is done.'

'He must have seen you coming.'

'Now will you take me to collect it on Saturday or not?'

The argument was lost. He knew it.

'Of course I will,' he grunted. 'But your father was right.'

'What about?'

'He said you'd never have any money as long as you had a hole in your backside.'

* * *

Harker sniffed and pulled a face like a bag of rhubarb. 'I hope you didn't upset him?' he said. 'He's an important man in Bromersley.'

Angel frowned. He didn't care if he had upset Chancey. And he wasn't important, just rich. 'There is no hard evidence to indicate foul play, sir: there's no ransom letter and no witnesses. Just Chancey's statement that she has disappeared, together with his instinct based upon what he claims is his intimate knowledge of his wife's behaviour.'

'What's your take on it?'

'There might very well be a case there, sir. He's in his thirties and has money to burn, and she's an active twenty-two-year-old model, been married two years and busier than rabbits in a hutch. She wears next to nothing and wears it very well. Chancey says she's a highly successful international model. If she is, she could be making more money than he is, so his money might count as nothing to her. I think until a ransom note arrives, a body turns up or a witness talks we should let him make his own enquiries. Let him waste his own money.'

Harker's bushy ginger eyebrows shot up. 'What's that? What's that about his own enquiries?'

'He said that if we don't start looking for her within a couple of days, he'll engage his own private detectives.'

Harker pulled a face more revolting than a Strangeways slop bucket. 'We can't have a load of amateurs under our feet, Angel. Better go back there. Assume the Chancey woman has been . . . abducted.'

'It's more likely she's run off with a new bloke, sir.'

'I daresay, but he wouldn't like that.'

'He wouldn't like murder any better.'

* * *

Angel returned to his office. He really didn't like this tiptoeing around Frank Chancey the way Harker wanted him to do it. He wanted to get into Wolff's filing cabinet. Who knew what evidence there might be stashed in there about the murderer? If he could get this annoying preliminary enquiry into the missing Katrina Chancey out of the way, he could get back to the real business of solving a murder case.

He reached out for the phone.

'Ahmed, get me Ron Gawber and Trevor Crisp ASAP. And get me the number of a model agency . . . it is called "Top Notch". They're in London.'

'Right, sir.'

A few moments later he was speaking on the phone to Melanie.

'Are you wanting a model or do you want to be on our books?' she said.

'Neither. I'm Detective Inspector Angel from the Bromersley force. I'm making enquiries about Katrina Chancey.'

'Oh yes.' She exploded with concern. 'Katrina. Yes. I see. Now what has happened to her, Inspector? She has let me down terribly. And I have not heard from her. There are jobs lining up for her. I have clients waiting and they don't like waiting. They want her and won't take substitutes. I really need to know what's happening.'

'Can't tell you that, Miss Melanie. I wish I knew.'

'Just Melanie, Inspector.'

'Right. I am looking to you to fill us in, Melanie. I need to know about her whereabouts from Saturday, the fourteenth of April.'

'So do I. I don't know. Her last job for me was on Tuesday the tenth of April with the Milo Advertising Agency, a photograph for the cover of a magazine. That went well, I understand. She had nothing then until Sunday the twenty-ninth, when she should have been at Heathrow at noon. She had an arrangement to meet up with a photographer and Max Peppino, to go on a shoot to the Maldives for three days for Elmer's Fruit Squashes. But it was a disaster. She didn't show up and she couldn't apparently be contacted. The client didn't know what to do. It was costing him his time and the photographer's time, which he valued at twelve hundred pounds a day! Huh! He was screaming down the phone at me. Anyway, I tried to contact Katrina on her mobile, but she wasn't answering. I tried her home number at various times through Sunday afternoon and evening, but couldn't make contact. I tracked down her husband's office number and managed to speak to him just after nine o'clock on Monday morning. He was very surprised and worried that she had missed the shoot. He told me he had thought she was in Rome, on holiday. He said that he would get her to contact me when she returned. But I haven't heard a word from her, or him. I don't know what Max Peppino did. I expect the shoot was abandoned that day. He must have used some other model from another agency and done it later without Katrina. And I fear I may have lost a client.'

'Sorry about that, Melanie. But thanks for the information. If you hear from her, or hear anything about her, it's imperative that you let me know at Bromersley Police. Will you do that?'

He gave her the station number and ended the conversation politely and quickly. After he had replaced the phone, he pulled a face. He had learned nothing that would be at all helpful in finding Katrina. Melanie had simply confirmed everything that Chancey had said, but that was all.

There was a knock at the door.

It was Ron Gawber. 'You wanted me, sir?'

'This woman, Katrina Chancey, husband of Frank Chancey, millionaire in the timber business, friend of the chief constable, has gone missing. Here's her credit-card numbers, bank account and mobile. See what activity there's been since the fourteenth of April, the day she was supposed to go to Rome.'

* * *

Angel stopped his BMW at the front entrance of Chancey's House. He got out of the car and looked around. The area in the middle of the square, where the concrete foundations of the marble fountain were being laid the day previously, was covered over with two canvas sheets like tenting and held down by eight house bricks. Also he noticed that a smart new red Ferrari was parked on the gravel where the ready-mix vehicles had been. He reflected on it briefly as he bounced up the four steps and pressed the doorbell.

He had to wait a few moments before the young man, Lyle, arrived at the door. He smiled down at the policeman. 'Back so soon, Inspector Angel? You'll be wanting to see Mr Chancey?'

'If you please, Mr Lyle.'

'I'll have a looksee. I do know the boss is going out imminently. Come in, please and wait yourself there.'

Behind the doors was a pillar projecting from the wall from the floor to the ceiling, boxed in with dark oak panelling. He pulled open a panel and inside was a phone. He unhooked the handset and tapped in a number. Angel heard a click and a distorted voice said, 'Yes?'

'There's Inspector Angel at the front door for you, boss.'

'Oh. All right, Jimmy. Just a couple of minutes.'

There was another click and Lyle put the phone back in its cradle and closed the panel door. He turned to Angel. 'Please follow me, Inspector. The boss said he's sorry, he's only got a couple of minutes because he's got a meeting at the office.'

Angel nodded. That was all right. It might suit him very well. They passed the big oil paintings again. They mostly showed ugly, elderly men with hunting rifles posed standing either on their own or with a handsome, sometimes buxom, woman. The artist had caught none of the subjects smiling;

in those times, in the US, they were usually painted scowling or glaring aggressively.

'These Mr Chancey's ancestors, Mr Lyle?'

The young man laughed. 'Sure. They look funny old coves, don't they, Inspector? Did you know Mr Chancey can trace his ancestors all the way back to before the gold rush of 1848 in the United States.'

'Really?' Angel said. Suddenly he could smell paint. He remembered he could smell paint yesterday. It was irritating.

Lyle ushered Angel into the room.

'Good morning, Inspector,' Chancey said. 'You must excuse me. I have to dash.'

'Indeed, sir. I wondered if you have heard anything at all about your wife?'

Chancey frowned.

'No, Inspector. If I had I would have contacted you straight away. Now I must go.'

Angel said, 'In your absence, perhaps I may look round the house.'

Chancey hesitated, then said, 'Yes, of course. Wherever you like, old chap.' He turned to Lyle. 'Jimmy, tell Mrs Symington, and let's get off.'

'Right, boss,' Lyle said and rushed out of the room.

'One more thing.'

'Yes?'

'Do you have a recent photograph of your dear wife, Mr Chancey. That would help us in our searches for her?'

Chancey breathed out impatience, but he pulled open the desk drawer and took out a photograph in a silver frame. 'Will that do? Taken three weeks ago, for a calendar for next year, I understand. Rather special. I'd like it back.'

'Of course, sir.' Angel glanced at it. 'Yes, that's fine.'

Chancey then turned the key in the middle drawer of his desk and put it in his pocket. He picked up a briefcase from the kneehole of the desk and made for the door.

'Must be off, Inspector. Glad to see you on the case. If you will wait there, I will send Mrs Symington, my house-manager to you.'

He was gone.

Angel looked carefully at the picture of Katrina that Chancey had given him. It was rather different from the racy photographs around the study walls. It was the sort of photograph you used to see in glass showcases outside theatres, to advertise the play being performed that night. It was a close-up, glossy print showing the young woman in a smart suit of immaculate appearance. Pencil-thin eyebrows, thick black eyelashes, clear blue eyes, pearl and diamond earrings, short blonde hair — and not one hair out of place; hands showing perfect fingernails and a big diamond solitaire ring on her right hand.

He stared at the photograph and rubbed his chin.

He heard the rustle of movement of clothes and the very lightest of footsteps on the carpet behind him. He turned round to find a sour-faced woman approaching him from the open door.

'I'm Mrs Symington, house-manager to Mr and Mrs Chancey. You must be Inspector Angel. I've been instructed to show you anything you want to see. You'll have to make it quick as I've a lot on, I can tell you. I didn't bargain on all this extra work and then playing the part of a guide to his visitors. I am a house-manager, not a flaming hostess.'

He turned and smiled at her.

'Thank you, Mrs Symington. I hope not to be a problem to you. But we all have our jobs to do. I would much rather be at home with my feet up, but I have to be here looking for a missing woman. I have to find where Mrs Chancey's got to. I am sorry if my job in any way inconveniences you. If you haven't the time to spare to show me what I need to see, I could, I suppose, manage on my own.'

Mrs Symington's face changed. Her mouth dropped open and then quickly closed. 'Oh, Mr Angel. Please forgive me. I didn't mean to be so rude. I don't know what got into me. But I have so much to see to, you wouldn't believe.'

'I would. I would, indeed. Now, Mr Chancey has gone. Please sit down, Mrs Symington. Rest those legs. I will only keep you a few minutes.'

She smiled. It looked as if she hadn't smiled for a long time. Angel found an easy chair and sat opposite her.

'There,' he said. 'That's more civilized, isn't it.'

'I haven't sat down since I had my breakfast at half past seven.'

'Now, what is the trouble? Tell me all about it.'

'Well, I didn't say there was any trouble. I've been in this job for nearly a year, Mr Angel, and it pays very well, I must say in fairness. Else I wouldn't stick it. It has been all right, until about two weeks ago. Mr Chancey called me in here and said that he wanted the house cleaning from top to bottom, that Mrs Chancey would be away for a fortnight or three weeks and in that time he wanted all the rooms repainting, all the carpets dry-cleaned, all his and her clothes laundered or dry cleaned. The kitchen and the bathroom tiles and surfaces had to be washed down with bleach. And the list went on. He said I could get extra staff in, if I needed them. Of course I needed them but I couldn't get any. Not for a temporary job. And what sort of people do you get as temporaries? He didn't seem to understand that. This house has been turned into a travelling circus. He says he wants everything spotless for when she returns. He misses her dreadfully, you see. I can tell. It's all for her. He's even had her Porsche taken away and a brand new hundred and sixty thousand pound Ferrari delivered. It's at the front entrance. Nothing is too good for her.'

Angel rubbed his chin. It explained why he could smell paint. 'And has everything been done?'

'No. He's building a gazebo in the grounds so that he can look out on Lord and Lady Tiverton in their garden and see what they're up to. At least that's what Jimmy Lyle says it's for. And there's going to be a marble fountain in the square at the front. It's going to be huge and will spout water all day out of a fish's mouth. It'll cost eighty thousand pounds. What do you think to that, Mr Angel?'

He frowned. He didn't know what to think of it. He pondered a moment. There were times when he would have liked to have shown his great passion and love of his dear wife, Mary, but it could never have amounted to anything like eighty thousand pounds. And he remembered that he would have to get that gas bill paid first.

'Would you like to start by showing me the kitchen?' he said.

'Would you like a cup of tea?'

'I thought you'd never ask.'

SEVEN

'I enjoyed that, Mrs Symington. Thank you. It's got rid of that smell of paint.'

'Put your cup in the bottom of the sink. It can go in the dishwasher later.'

'Have the painters finished?'

'Yes. Finished yesterday.'

'Is everything else done?

'Just about. My staff have finished bleach washing the bathrooms and in here. Can't you smell it?'

He thought he could, but it wasn't obvious. The smell of paint was predominant.

'The laundry has come back,' she said. 'The dry-cleaning is back. There are men still steam-cleaning the carpets in the guest bedrooms. They should have finished the other day but they are nearly through. Where would you like to start? What exactly do you want to see?'

'I don't know, Mrs Symington. Everything, I suppose. I only know when I see it.'

She showed him the downstairs rooms, which were — as he'd come to expect — outrageously luxurious. He saw the patio with the Spanish outdoor furniture and the colourful parasol by the side of the swimming pool. She was directing him through the front hall where there was a big log fire in full blaze. As he passed it he felt no warmth from it at all.

He returned to it and stared at the flame flickering from the artificial logs and the red glowing cinders.

She watched him and smiled.

After a moment Angel said, 'I thought it was the real thing.'

'Everybody does.'

'Does it get hot at all?'

'Oh yes,' she said. 'There's a thermostat up here.' She pointed to a dial on a small control box hardly visible at the side of the chimney breast. 'If you turn the thermostat at the side here, real gas flames come up, it'll warm the place up a bit, but, of course, it isn't intended to burn anything. And we always seem to feel warm enough in this house.'

Angel nodded.

'If you follow me, we can take a look round upstairs,' she said.

He nodded.

It was as sumptuous, spotless and magnificent as it was downstairs. The Chanceys' dressing-room, off their bedroom, had wardrobes stuffed with clothes. When she opened Katrina's wardrobe Mrs Symington pointed to the vast array of shoes. 'Mr Chancey went really wild, you know,' she said. 'He threw all her old shoes away. Every pair. These are all new. Look at them. He knows that she is really crazy about shoes. Shortly after she went away, he came up here and took all her shoes.'

Angel blinked. 'All of them? Well, how many pairs were there?'

'I don't know, but a lot.'

'What did he do with them?'

'Threw them away.'

He sighed.

'She would sometimes change her shoes six times in a day. He knew that. He went out and bought thirty-six *new* pairs of shoes, just like that. Some of them are famous names. Cost the earth.'

Angel leaned forward and picked up a red leather shoe from a pair. He bounced one of them thoughtfully in his hand. He looked inside. He saw a figure '3'. He put it back, then picked up a single black shoe, similar to the red. He bounced that in the same way and looked inside. He blinked as he read off the figure. It was a '6'.

Mrs Symington saw him react. 'What's the matter, Inspector.'

'Different size.'

She frowned. 'Different size?' she said, taking it from him and looking inside it.

'Yes,' he said leaning down to the other new shoes on the shoe rail on the wardrobe floor. He kept picking up a shoe, checking inside for its size, calling out its size, discarding it and picking up another.

Mrs Symington joined in and was calling out numbers in the range from '2' to '8'.

'They do make pairs, I believe,' she said.

He agreed. 'Yes, but they won't all fit Mrs Chancey, that's for sure.' He put the last shoe down and ran his hand through his hair. 'Beats me,' he said.

She shook her head. 'Whatever was Mr Chancey thinking about?'

He turned to Mrs Symington and said, 'Is there anybody who deals specifically with her clothes?'

73

'Yes. Of course, Inspector. There's Maria.'

She found a phone hanging conveniently on the wall in the dressing-room. She picked it up and summoned a young woman to the master bedroom. She introduced her and told Angel that in more normal times, Maria worked part-time. She attended to Mrs Chancey's clothes, and cleaned and maintained the upstairs rooms and bathrooms. However, during the last two weeks she had put in many extra hours, as everybody else had, to accommodate Mr Chancey's wish to make everything spotless, clean and shiny in preparation for his wife's return.

'Did you put these shoes here in the wardrobe, Maria?' Angel said.

The young woman gaped down at the heap of untidy shoes on the floor. She wasn't pleased.

'Here, what you been doing with all them Miss Katrina's shoes?'

'What size is Mrs Chancey?' Angel said. 'These sizes are over the place.'

'I noticed that,' Maria said. 'I don't know what happened there. It was a delivery from Hemingford's. You knows that, Mrs Symington?'

Hemingford's was a luxury department store in Leeds. The Chanceys were frequent customers of the establishment.

'That is so,' Mrs Symington said. 'They all came together in one carton. Mr Chancey told me thirty-six pairs of shoes were to be delivered. He said they were to go straight into his wife's wardrobe, so when their van delivered it, I got Mr Lyle to bring the box upstairs, and I told Maria, and that's all I know.'

Maria said, 'And that's all I know too. I opened the box, put the shoes in the wardrobe properly, in pairs. There were thirty-six pairs, and I took the empty boxes down to the paper-recycling bin in the back kitchen. What's wrong with that?'

Angel rubbed his chin, dropped his head on one side, looked at Maria and smiled. 'Nothing, Maria,' he said. 'Nothing at all. I have to ask these questions. I don't like it any more than you do, but it's my job. All right?'

She shrugged.

Angel said, 'Were you here when Mrs Chancey packed to leave for Rome?'

'No,' Maria said. 'That was on a Saturday. Must have been late. I finish at noon on Saturdays. Sorry.'

'Do you know what clothes she took?'

'Oh yes,' she said. 'I checked it against what she left behind. She must have packed in a hurry. She took three suits . . . they would be very hot in Rome, I would have thought, at this time of year, though, some blouses, tops, silver brush and comb set, almost all her make-up, and her silver sandals.'

Angel pursed his lips. 'Anything else?'

'Well,' Maria said with a grin. She looked down at the carpet. 'I don't know if I should mention it . . .' She put a hand in front of her mouth.

Mrs Symington's eyes shot up and then down again quickly.

'What's that?' she snapped.

'Well, she didn't take no underwear, nor any nightdresses,' Maria said, her big eyes glancing from the house-manager to the policeman and back.

Mrs Symington glanced at Angel to see how he had taken this potentially embarrassing intelligence.

Angel's face was as straight as a bobby's truncheon. It wasn't difficult. There was very little left to surprise him. He couldn't care less what Katrina Chancey wore or didn't wear in bed, on a catwalk or anywhere else. But he was not a happy bunny. Although he now accepted that Katrina Chancey hadn't gone to Rome, he was no nearer finding out where she *had* gone, with whom and, indeed, where she was at that present time.

* * *

'There's no evidence, sir,' Angel said. 'That's the problem.'

Harker sniffed, withdrew the white plastic menthol inhaler from out of his colossal red nose, replaced the cap, thrust it into his pocket and said, 'Because, according to her gormless maid, a woman didn't take the clothes which were appropriate for a holiday in Rome in April, it doesn't necessarily mean that she didn't go there.'

Angel sighed and said, 'Well she didn't arrive at the Hotel Leonardo Quincento in Rome, where her husband had booked for her; she didn't fly on flight 183A from Leeds/Bradford to Heathrow and catch flight 221 Heathrow to Rome, which her husband had bought tickets for; and we are unable to discover any local taxi service, private hire car, bus, or friend who collected her from the house and delivered her to the airport that Saturday morning.'

Harker's face changed. 'Oh? You've checked it all out?'

'Everything, sir. And according to her husband, her own car was still in the garage at the house. So she didn't drive herself.'

'Well, there's only one conclusion to be drawn then, isn't there? She's hopped off with a boyfriend and is living it up in some love-nest or discreet hotel somewhere.'

Angel frowned and bit his bottom lip.

'Aye,' Harker continued. 'And somewhere where the climate is not as hot as in Rome.'

Angel wasn't at all sure about that, but he had a murder case to deal with, and while he was messing about looking for the wife of a friend of the chief's, a killer was running around scot free.

'Are you happy to tell the chief that then, sir?'

Harker pulled a face. Angel could see he was far from happy about it. Mind you, he would have said that it was difficult to remember anything Harker had ever been happy about. He watched him. He really was an ugly man. He could have modelled masks for Halloween.

At length Harker sighed and rubbed his hand across his mouth.

Angel said, 'I've still got a murder case on my hands, sir. That wig maker. I need to get back to that. I don't want it going cold on me.'

'Aye. All right. All right. I'll tell him. I don't know quite what I'll tell him, but I'll tell him.' He sniffed and rubbed his bony chin.

'You can tell him that without a ransom note, or a witness of foul play or her dead body, we can't do—'

'All right. All right. If I want a bloody scriptwriter, I'll hire one.'

* * *

Angel came out of the superintendent's office and stormed down the green corridor. Harker always managed to make him angry; he must have had a degree in cussedness and taken extra lessons in annoyance. Anyway, Angel was relieved to be able to concentrate on finding Peter Wolff's murderer.

As he passed the CID room Ahmed saw him whiz by and ran behind him all the way to his office.

At the door, Angel turned round, saw him and said, 'Now Ahmed, what is it lad?'

'Came in the post, sir,' Ahmed said, waving an envelope. 'Addressed to you.'

Angel took it and opened it while still on the move into his office. He nodded to Ahmed to close the door.

Inside the envelope was a postcard-size photograph of a suit of armour. Angel's head came up; he had forgotten all about Lord Tiverton's missing suit of armour, so much had happened. He turned the photograph over: it was perfectly blank. He turned it back again; the armour looked very heavy, black and cumbersome.

'Ahmed. Get that copied and distributed to all forty-three forces. Send a copy to my mate at the Art and Antiques unit, DI Matthew Elliott. With the caption, 'stolen last month', and a note to say that if anybody knows anything about it to contact me at any time and give my mobile number. All right? If it's on the market, looking for a buyer, it'll turn up.'

'Right, sir,' Ahmed said and turned away.

Angel called him back. 'Ahmed! Find DS Crisp for me. I don't know where that lad gets to.'

'Yes, sir,' Ahmed said, and rushed out.

Angel sighed and rubbed his chin. He looked round and began to wonder where to begin.

The phone rang. He picked it up. 'Angel.'

It was a young PC on reception.

'SOCO are here with a filing cabinet for you, sir. They say it's very heavy. Full of papers. They want to know where you want them to put it.'

Angel looked round his little office. In the corner by the stationery cupboard was an ordinary police-issue chair, used only when he had more than one visitor at a time. He could soon sling that out. 'Bring it down here,' he said. 'In my office. I'll show them where.'

He replaced the phone, rubbed his chin, picked the phone up again and dialled a number.

'Mac? Michael Angel. How you doing with that postmortem on Peter Wolff?'

'The practical's done. Just got to tidy up my notes and have them typed out.'

'I'll come round.'

After he'd had the filing cabinet safely delivered into his office Angel drove across the town to Bromersley general hospital. And found his way to the mortuary.

It was a brightly lit, white tiled mausoleum behind locked doors. Although he had been there many times he never got used to the smell of ammonia and body fluids, the hum of refrigeration motors and regular rattle of metal fan belt covers, the sound of flushing water, cisterns filling and the minions in green overalls and masks flitting silently around with buckets and hosepipes. It was not the stagey glamour and sophistication seen on television.

He made his way across narrow drains and wet tiled floors to Mac's tiny office.

'Come in, Michael,' the Scotsman said.

'Thank you, Mac,' Angel said. He tugged the long switch-cord for the fan as he passed it. 'No objection to fresh air, have we?' He nodded up at the Vent-Axia in the sloping glass ceiling high above them.

'I get used to it.'

Angel's nose wrinkled up. He never would.

'Sit down. There's not much to tell.'

Angel took the chair and waited.

Mac reached out for a file. He opened it and began to read.

'Peter Wolff. Height: Five feet, eleven inches tall. Weight: eleven stones, two pounds. Age: thought to be between forty-five and fifty years.'

'What did he die of, Mac?'

'Gunshot wound to the heart.'

'How many shots?'

'Just the one. A .202. A handgun, I should think, fired only a few inches away. His chest, the quilt and sheet covered in powder.'

'Any signs of a struggle? Any other wounds?'

'No. None. It looks as if he was unaware of the approach of any intruder. He was shot and died instantly.'

'Nothing else? Anything interesting under his fingernails, for instance?'

'Fragments of cheese. He seemed to have had a cheese sandwich or something with cheese in it four to six hours before death.'

'Anything interesting in his stomach . . . any booze in his blood?'

Mac pursed his lips and shook his head. 'No.'

'Any needle marks anywhere?'

'No. And before you ask, he didn't smoke either.'

Angel stroked his chin and sighed.

Mac said, 'I told you there wasn't much.'

'If Pope John Paul had still been alive, this man would have been made a saint?'

EIGHT

Angel got into the BMW and pointed the bonnet out of the hospital car park. His chat with Dr Mac had in no way progressed his investigation into the murder of Peter Wolff. The postmortem seemed to have told him nothing at all useful. He recalled that his last few cases had had no great proliferation of forensic clues. Twenty years ago, you could have expected the occasional clear fingerprint on a gun or a knife or a broken bottle that would make a case easy, and ensure a guilty verdict as predictably as a traffic speed camera catching you on your night out!

He hoped that SOCO were going to come up with something helpful. He was going to chivvy them up just as soon as he got into the office.

He turned left into Rotherham Road and was sailing along Main Street, where stood the Feathers, Bromersley's only salubrious three-star hotel. As he was coming up to the hotel entrance he saw a familiar figure, big green hat, light-coloured raincoat, collar and tie, leaning against the door arch on the steps. It was Irish John. He hadn't seen him in a couple of years or more. There he was, Ireland's export to Britain, coolly rolling a cigarette.

Angel suddenly had an idea.

He pushed both feet down on to the pedals; there was a screech of brakes, he banged the indicator light stalk down, checked his mirror, and then pulled the steering wheel hard right pointing the car bonnet straight between two stone pillars into the Feathers car park.

By the time Angel had locked the car and reached the hotel entrance, Irish John — John Corcoran to HMP Armley and others — had disappeared. Angel turned round and walked back to the end of the frontage of the hotel and took a quick sideways step round the corner. He waited there, trying not to seem impatient, looking at his watch. Exactly five minutes later Irish John came out of the hotel, looking like a rabbit coming out its hole into the daylight. He looked round cautiously; not seeing Angel, he dipped into his pocket and pulled out the spindly thin and misshapen excuse for a cigarette and stuck it in his mouth. He found a match, lit it, inhaled, then pulled the cigarette away and began coughing. He coughed and coughed. He went red in the face. His red eyes stuck out. He held the offending weed dangling and smouldering between his shaking fingers as he coughed and spluttered. He had found his disgraceful handkerchief and was holding it to his mouth as he coughed.

Angel heard it. He couldn't help but hear it. He came out of hiding from round the side of the hotel and made a beeline for the Irishman.

When Corcoran saw him his watery eyes flashed like a frightened cat's.

'John Corcoran,' Angel said with a smile.

'I haven't done notting,' the Dubliner said in an accent you could cut with a forged Visa card. 'I'm as innocent as a newborn babe, Inspector Angel. You haven't got notting on me.'

He had stopped coughing. It must have been the shock of seeing Angel.

'Buy you a drink, John?'

Corcoran looked stunned. His face slowly brightened when he realized he was not about to be arrested.

'For old times' sake?' Angel added.

Corcoran smiled. 'To clear de troat, that would be vaary acceptable, Inspector. Tank you.'

They went through the revolving doors and turned right into the public bar. The place was deserted so they were served promptly: a Guinness for Corcoran and a bottle of German beer for Angel. They sat in one of the partly curtained cubicles for four, and looked across the table at each other.

'How long you been out?' Angel said.

'Ah. We not going to be talking about my stay at Her Majesty's pleasure, are we, Inspector? You didn't coax me into this glorious alcoholic palace to talk to me about my holidays, did you?'

Angel smiled and sipped the beer.

Corcoran leaned forward and said quietly, 'If you really must know, I did ten months in Armley, then moved for a year to Lincoln and then six months at Boston, which according to my mattemattics means I come out two weeks ago today.'

'And have you found a job yet? Is the probation office doing its stuff?'

'Well I don't know about that. I went down to the "Labour" and they went through my qualifications and stuff and at first, they could only offer me a job on the bins. Well I have niver been so insulted. Then there was a vacancy driving a forklift. That sounded like real hard work, moving timber around for eight hours a day. My back won't stand that sort of abuse, Inspector Angel. I prefer something more . . . more in keeping with my . . . breeding and education. There's a driving job going, driving a big nob round, it's only temporary, they said. I would have to wear a uniform. So I have to go for an interview for that, tomorrow morning, I think it was.'

Angel shook his head. 'Did you always take so long to answer a simple question, John?'

'It's on account of my being married once, you know, Inspector. Oh yes. Many moons ago now, I'm glad to say.'

'Didn't know you'd been married.'

'Oh, Inspector. In those long and dark days the thing was, if you became aware of a silence, then that was the time to start saying what you had to say, and to keep going and get it out of your system until you were interrupted, which in her mother's house didn't take very long at all, I can tell you.'

'I'll take that as a yes. Did you and your wife not have your own house when you got married, then?'

'Oh yes. Her mudder promised to give a house to her loving daughter Maureen and myself on the day the connubials was blessed with child.'

'So you were a year or so before . . . you got a house?'

'No sir. Two weeks. In fact, she was rushed to the doctor's straight after the connubials. The wedding dress was too tight round the . . . middle, you understand. And the excitement and the booze and that. And do you know,' he said, lowering his voice to a whisper. 'I was denied the matrimonial bed and the conjugals until three weeks after we were married!'

'But you got the house?'

'Oh yes. Oh yes, Inspector. Oh yes. I got the house, the bed, the furniture, the bills, the wife, the baby, *and* the mother-in-law. It was just too much for a poor, simple man, to acquire all at once. So I waited a full week — that was a respectable length of time, I thought — and then I hoofed it away. I thought that some other poor bastard down on his luck could have the pleasure of Maureen and her mother. A readymade home for him to walk straight into, if you see what I mean. Don't you think that I did the right thing, Inspector Angel?'

Angel stifled a smile. 'If you *let* her divorce *you* and paid maintenance of the baby.'

'What! I should cocoa. The baby wasn't mine. Would you believe it? It came out that it was the mother-in-law's lodger who had had that honour. And he was quick to move on. And years later, after her mother died, the old witch, Maureen got caught up with a metal-basher from Cork who could give her all she needed. Well, that's what she said. Anyway she needed a quiet divorce from myself so that she could tie the connubials with him. This was quite a few years ago now. So we agreed most amicably to a divorce. But Maureen wouldn't divorce in Dublin. Oh no. She said it wasn't respectable. It should be done in an English court. Out of the way, you know. Strict Roman Catholic she was. So I brought her over to Liverpool. Stayed in a boarding house down Islington Road. Tell you what, Inspector Angel. We made up for the conjugals we couldn't have between the wedding and the birth of Brigid. Anyway, we went before the judge and pleaded on the grounds of incompatibility. Incompatibility! I told the judge that I thought that that was putting it mildly and do you know what, Inspector?'

Angel shook his head.

'He fined me ten pounds for contempt of court!'

Corcoran took a good gulp of the Guinness, then he shut one eye, lowered his voice and said, 'But you've got me jabbering, and that's not what it's about. What is it you're wanting from me, Inspector?'

'Information, John. For money.'

'What sort of money? Would it be enough to get me legless?'

'Probably. You see, John, I've got a dead body on my hands and I can't find who killed him. He was shot in the heart close up.'

Corcoran's eyes flashed. His hands went up and came down. 'Just a minute, Inspector. This is Irish John you're talking to. You know I don't do shooters. I don't go anywheres near shooters. That's porridge long time. Strictly not for me. I keeps away from wild men with shooters.'

'I know that, and I'm not going to ask you anything about the murderer. I want to know about the victim.'

'Oh. Aaaah!' he said agreeably.

'His name is Peter Wolff and he was a wig maker. He had a shop at thirty-eight Market Street. Does it mean anything to you?'

'A wig maker?' Corcoran said. He lifted his glass, emptied it and lowered it to the table noisily. Angel pointed at it, Corcoran nodded and said, 'It's my turn.'

'I'll do it,' Angel said. He stood up, took the glasses to the bar and returned with the same again.

He placed the Guinness in front of Corcoran.

'I been thinking, Inspector. To tell the truth I niver heard of him. A wig maker. Don't like the sound of it. Messing with other people's hair. No. Peter Wolff, did you say? And he's been *murdered*?'

'Ask around will you? There's a bit of money in it for you.'

* * *

Angel reached his office at ten minutes to five. He immediately reached out for the phone and tapped in SOCO's number. He eventually reached Don Taylor.

'I'm still waiting for your report on Peter Wolff's place, Don?'

'It's almost ready, sir. A bit difficult and unusual, what the fire didn't damage, the water did.'

'I was looking to you to throw me a lifeline.'

'Nothing very direct, sir. No fingerprints, no footprints, no bodily fluids. No DNA. Only the victim's.'

He rubbed his chin and licked his bottom lip. 'Wasn't there *any*thing?'

'Yes, sir. Very unusual. Splashes of a metal, mainly on the floor in the shop and the back room downstairs, and taken by treading and being carried on Woolf's footwear to the two upper floors. There were traces on his slippers and his shoes. It's almost as if there was some sort of a metal repair business being carried on downstairs.'

'What sort of metal?'

'We have to make sure, sir, but initial tests indicate that the dust is a high grade of gold. And some platinum.'

Angel frowned. That *was* unusual. He felt a warm vibration in his chest. This investigation was getting interesting. 'When will you know?'

'I'll check it out with the laboratory at Wetherby, sir. I'll send one of the victim's shoes. A couple of days or so.'

'Right. Anything else?'

'There is one item we couldn't deal with. That might prove helpful.'

'What's that?'

'There's a huge safe on the ground floor, under the stairs leading to the first floor. It's bricked in, amateurishly, but

87

strongly. Probably did it himself. It was hidden behind a hinged panel. All clever stuff. We can't open it with the kit we've got, and the keys weren't anywhere on the premises.'

'Searched his pockets?'

'Oh yes, sir. Found a bunch of keys for the shop and that. Thing is, the safe is an old Castle Mark II. Big job. It needs two keys with extra-long shanks. Might be ten or fifteen inches long or even longer. We've searched everywhere. And I mean *every*where?'

Angel knew how thorough SOCO were. If they search a place, they pull floorboards up, remove tiles, knock walls down if necessary, bring sniffer dogs in, use heat-seeking equipment, X-ray techniques. If something had been hidden they would always find it.

'Have to bring in a locksmith from Castles.'

'That might take a few days. Is there a serial number on it?'

'Yes, sir.'

'Have you finished dusting it?'

'Yes, sir. Just Wolff's dabs on it, sir.'

'Is someone from uniform still on duty at Wolff's shop?'

'Oh yes, sir.'

'Better put them on their mettle, Don.'

As Angel replaced the phone he was thinking he didn't want someone with the keys, the murderer perhaps, who could have stolen them the night of the murder, calling back there to help himself to the contents of Wolff's safe. He couldn't imagine what was in there. Taylor had said it was a big safe . . . Wigs, hair, cash? Something that was going to pin-point Wolff's murderer? He grunted aloud. He would have to wait until tomorrow. It was five o'clock. Might as well call it a day.

* * *

Angel was in bed, Mary next to him, both asleep. A distant clock chimed. Angel suddenly woke up. He blinked several times. The bedroom was as black as an undertaker's hat. He peered at the luminous clock dial on the bedside table. It was two o'clock. He lay still there a moment listening to his own breathing. Then he listened to Mary's. It was regular, slow and peaceful. He sat up in bed and scratched his stomach. Something had disturbed him. He usually slept like a well-fed Labrador. He noticed his heart was beating faster than usual. Then it came to him in a flash. It was something that had been bothering him all evening. He simply couldn't shake off thinking about the concealed safe at Peter Wolff's shop, and how the contents might throw light on the identity of his murderer. He gently peeled back the sheet; he didn't want to disturb Mary. He put his feet on the pink carpet and fumbled around for his slippers.

Twelve minutes later, he was dressed — in a fashion — and was driving his car into the almost empty park at the rear of Bromersley police station. He let himself in the rear door with his card, dashed up the deserted corridor to his office . . . switched on the light and made a beeline to Wolff's filing cabinet standing in the corner.

He had been thinking. Logically, at the time of Peter Wolff's murder, the keys to the safe had to have been on the victim's premises. Where else would they have been? SOCO hadn't found them, so they couldn't have been there at the time of the search. Therefore they had to have been removed by the murderer or by the police. The only items authorized to be taken from the premises were Wolff's body and the green filing cabinet. Clearly SOCO would have searched the body, so unless the murderer had taken them with the intention of returning, the only remaining logical place for the keys to be was in the filing cabinet.

Angel purposefully snatched open the three drawers one by one. Each of the drawers, which glided out on runners, was packed with thin green cardboard files suspended on rails and labelled by tags that projected an inch or so from the top of each file. Systematically and carefully he pulled out handfuls of files and their contents from each drawer to see if either of the two unusual-looking keys had been concealed underneath the files in the bottom of the drawer. There was no luck in the top two drawers, but when he lifted files out of the bottom drawer, there, staring at him, were two keys about fourteen inches long. They had a flat castle motif at the end of each key, so he was positive that they must be the ones. His heart missed a beat as he snatched them up, stuffed them into his raincoat pocket, where they protruded precariously. He replaced the files carefully and precisely, closed all the drawers and dashed out of the station.

He hardly noticed the quietness of the yellow-illuminated, deserted streets and the eeriness of the night. His mind was exclusively concentrated on the contents and possible evidence that might be revealed if he was able to open Wolff's safe.

He stopped the BMW outside 38 Market Street. The wig shop still had blue on white DO NOT CROSS tape across the black burned frontage.

He glanced round for the uniformed policeman who should have been on high profile duty to keep looters and Nosy Parkers and anyone else away. He saw the glow of a cigarette end in the shadow of the covered doorway of the greetings card shop next door to Wolff's. The red glow suddenly disappeared as a uniformed constable stepped forward.

'Can I help you, sir,' a deep voice said.

'It's DI Angel, lad. Who are you?'

'Oh. Good evening, or is it good morning, sir? It's John Weightman. Is everything all right?'

Angel was pleased. He knew the constable very well indeed. He was one of the oldest and was also considered to be one of the most reliable men on Bromersley force.

'Yes, fine, John.'

'Something urgent on, sir?'

'Not exactly urgent. No. A development, you could say, just come to a head,' Angel said, making for the shop door. 'Is it locked?'

'No sir.'

'I need some light. Follow me inside and bring your torch.'

Weightman shone the powerful flashlight as Angel pushed open the glass door. Everything was black. The water had drained away from the floor, leaving burnt linoleum and scorched paintwork.

Angel wrinkled his nose. There was a fusty smell. Reminded him of latrines in Strangeways that were discovered to be bunged up with old pin-ups of Heather Mills.

He picked his way to the place under the stairs that Taylor had described to him. The hinged L-shaped partition was now standing an inch or so from the wall. Angel put his hands round the edges of the panel and pulled the partition away. It swung towards him on its hinges to reveal its secret.

'Shine your torch on here, John,' Angel said, looking at the green-painted safe with its copper-coloured identity tag, brass handle and keyholes.

'Ooo. Didn't know *that* was there.'

'Castle Mark II. You won't come across many of those,' Angel said, looking for the two keyholes. He found them easily enough. They were made in a coppery-looking metal, vertically set, one above the other and about six inches apart.

He pulled the keys out of his pocket. 'Shine your light on these, John,' he said.

'My goodness, sir. Never seen keys that long.'

'They'll go right into the metal casing. Prevents jellymen and lockpicks alike.'

Angel looked to see if there was any indication as to which key was for which keyhole. Near the flat Castle logo on the shank of one key was stamped a letter U, and on the other in the same place, the letter L. Upper and lower, he guessed. He inserted the keys, one at a time, pushed them all the way in, leaving only an inch and the finger grip with the logo on it sticking out, and then turned them. They each made a satisfying clunk. He reached out for the brass handle, pressed it down, pulled it towards him and the heavy safe door silently opened.

'Let me borrow your torch, John.'

Angel peered eagerly into the safe. It was ram-jammed full, packed as tightly and neatly as a watch.

There were three shelves. The top shelf was stuffed with paper money, twenty-pound notes in elastic bands, they seemed to be. The paper money extended to the back of the safe, as far as he could see. There must have been many thousands of pounds there.

'Good heavens!' Weightman said with a whistle. 'Aladdin's cave!'

'Aye. Careful not to touch anything inside the safe, John. SOCO have to do their stuff there yet.'

He shone the torch on the middle shelf. This was stuffed tightly with sixty or more small cardboard boxes; on the end of each box was a neat handwritten label. He could read:

diamonds, emeralds, rubies, pearls, opals, turquoise, amber, 9 ct jump rings, 18 ct chain, 18 ct jump rings and so on. On the floor of the safe, Angel could make out the diamond laden tips of a tiara half-wrapped with what seemed to be a ginger wig, on top of which was a plastic mask.

Angel felt a warm glow in his chest; a tremor of excitement made his hands shake briefly and his heart began to thump. This was quite a coup.

'Peter Wolff must have been the Fox, John.'

'The Fox? Really, sir? The wig maker?'

'There's his wig and mask and—'

'Wow! Thank goodness, sir,' the big man replied smiling. 'That's an end to that. Whatever will the papers write about now?'

Angel stood back from the safe, sighed, reluctantly closed it, locked it and withdrew both keys.

NINE

Angel pulled out the address book in his desk drawer, found the number he wanted, picked up the phone and dialled the number. It rang out. It kept ringing out. It seemed to be ringing for an interminably long time. He looked at his watch. It was 6 a.m. He cast his eyes round the office and then beyond, out through the window. As he listened to the monotonous brrr brrr, brr brr, he noticed the early morning sunlight dancing lightly on the yellowy-green leaves of the silver birch in the garden of the insurance company offices next door. He suddenly realized that maybe winter was really over, and that that day promised to be sunny, maybe the actual beginning of a glorious summer.

There was still no reply and he was about to drop the phone back in its cradle when there was a click and a half-awake man's voice from out of the side of his mouth, the other side being covered in pillow, grunted, 'Yeah? Yeah? What is it?'

'Good morning, Matthew. Michael Angel, Bromersley, here. The Fox is dead, Matthew. I thought you'd like to know.'

'What? The Fox is dead?'

'Yes. And it's a beautiful May morning. The sun is shining. The birds are coughing. Summer is on its way.'

'Have you seen the bloody time, Michael?'

'I have been up half the night.'

'You've not rung up about that suit of armour, have you? Did you say the Fox was dead?'

'Yes and we have found its lair. A thumping big safe overflowing with precious stones, diamonds, emeralds, rubies, sapphires, gold, a diamond tiara—'

'Where?' the interruption came quickly. 'Where?'

Angel knew he had the man's full attention. He was talking to DI Matthew Elliott, head of the Antiques and Fine Art squad, Scotland Yard. He had known him for years. Elliott would be able to assist him in trying to identify the victims of the Fox's robberies, which might, he hoped, lead to his murderer.

'I'll come up this morning.'

Angel smiled and replaced the phone.

* * *

'That's all very well, but we are still no nearer knowing who murdered him,' Harker said with a sniff.

'But it opens up a wider field of suspects, sir.'

'What do you mean?'

'Motive, sir,' Angel said. 'I had not been able to find a motive. I mean, who would want to have murdered Peter Wolff, a humble, quiet, apparently respectable wig maker? What harm could a wig maker do to a customer? What threat does a wig maker pose? What double-dealing could a wig maker get up to? Nothing that I can think of. I can't think of anything that would motivate a man to break into his place, creep up the stairs, shoot him while he was asleep and then set fire to his place. Now that we know he's the Fox, it's an entirely different proposition, isn't it?'

Harker sniffed. He seemed to agree but looked unenthused by it all.

'Well, sir,' Angel continued, 'there are all the jewellers he robbed; there's the competition from other thieves who may have been casing a shop just as he cleaned it out before them; there are the bullion dealers, stone dealers, auctioneers and jewellery manufacturers he may have sold to; there are the insurance companies who had to pay out millions in clients' claims; lastly, there is the fence he may have sold stuff through. Any one of them might hold a grudge against him.'

Harker sniffed. 'Maybe. That means you've plenty to be going at then, lad?'

Angel took it as his cue to leave. He stood up.

'Before you go, you'd better tell me how things stand with you and the search for Frank Chancey's wife?'

Angel's head shot up. 'You agreed I should leave it, sir. Yesterday you were going to tell the chief constable that there were no—'

'I know what I was *probably* going to do. I am asking you where the enquiry has got up to?'

'It has moved on no further, sir. No ransom note, no direct information of her abduction, no witness of foul play, no emergence of her actual dead body. You agreed yesterday, she was just a . . . misper.'

The corners of Harker's mouth turned down again. He drew in a deep breath and then blew it out.

Angel thought that he was under some pressure that he didn't want to speak about.

'If you still want me to pursue it, sir, I have a suggestion to make,' Angel said.

'Aye?'

'I've been thinking. The relationship between Chancey and his wife may not have been that cosy. After all, she left on Saturday, the fourteenth of April ostensibly for Rome, but he apparently didn't try to contact her by phone or any other way until sixteen days later, the thirtieth. We know *that* because, as she didn't in fact go to Rome, he didn't know that until sixteen days later, which means that at no time in that period had he phoned Rome to try to reach her. For that matter, she had not phoned him to tell him where she was. But maybe he wouldn't even have phoned on the thirtieth, if the model agency hadn't phoned him, concerned that Katrina had missed an appointment and couldn't make contact with her. To some couples it might seem to be a long time to be separated without so much as a phone call.'

'Hmmm,' Harker said rubbing his chin. 'True. True.'

Angel nodded. 'Under the circumstances, it would be very reasonable to ask him about his relationship with her. And it would get me back in his house, talking to him. You never know where it might lead.'

'There's a fair difference in their ages, isn't there?'

'She's twenty-two and he's thirty-seven.'

Harker sighed. 'Aye. Do it, lad. As soon as maybe. But don't upset him. He's a highly respected pillar of the community.'

* * *

'You're lucky to catch me, Inspector. I am usually at my office by this time. Anyway, now that you're here, what do you want? If you had any good news about Katrina, I expect you would not be standing there with an expression like that.'

Angel smiled and nodded gently.

'Oh, I am forgetting my manners,' Chancey continued. 'Please sit down. Would you like tea, or coffee . . . or anything?'

'No thank you, sir. And no, I regret that we have no new specific lines of enquiry, but there is just one thing that . . . bothers me.'

'Speak out, Inspector,' Chancey said looking directly at him across the big desk.

Angel knew he had to pick his words carefully. 'Well, you told me that your wife left early Saturday morning, the fourteenth of April?'

'Yes. That's right, as far as I know. I was actually at the office — where I should be now. What is wrong with that?'

'And that as far as you knew, at the time, she arrived safely in Rome, Italy, later that day.'

'Yes and booked into the very best hotel in that beautiful city. She adored the place. She has been there before. I have stayed there with her. I was satisfied that she would have been comfortable and happy there. Yes. Yes. What about it?'

'Yet, although you believed that she was happily enjoying her holiday there, you didn't *know* that, and it was sixteen days before you bothered to contact her. And that was precipitated by a rather desperate phone call to you from her model agency advising you that they could not reach her and that she had missed a vital appointment.'

'That's true. But I thought she would be happy to lounge around the pool, or go out on a shopping spree from time to time. She always enjoyed that. And I have been very busy with the house improvements, you know . . . the spring-cleaning, the fountain, and so on. I have also bought her a new car. I've made all these improvements for *her*, you know, Inspector. Not for me. Frankly, I could live in a box provided it wasn't noisy, was warm and it had a bit of a view with a few trees. But she likes everything smart and new and bright. I thought she would be over the moon when she returned. Besides all this extra work here, I have also been running a public company, you know, with twenty-two branches employing over eight hundred employees. And, incidentally, I am pleased to say that we are on course to announce a record profit for the half-year figures in June. I have been and still am a very, very busy man.'

'Isn't it true, Mr Chancey,' Angel said gently and carefully, 'that your marriage, to put it in the vernacular, was on the rocks?'

Chancey's jaw dropped. He looked away. It was as if he'd been hit on the side of the head with a Group Four prison bus. He breathed in and then out unevenly several times. It took a few moments for him to recover. Eventually he turned back to Angel and said quietly, 'How very clever of you, Inspector. I had heard that you were a highly perceptive policeman, and that . . . like the Mountie, you always got your man.'

Angel remained silent. He wasn't used to compliments. He didn't get many. He didn't say anything, just looked across the desk and waited.

'Very well. I'd better tell you something about how things were . . . and what happened that Friday night.'

Angel settled back in the chair, his pen at the ready.

'Katrina and I have only been married two years. I am keen to have children. I need a son, or more than one, to take over the business for one thing, although a daughter — or more than one — would be . . . delightful. Anyway, Katrina had said she agreed with me. That we both wanted children was absolutely great. I was eagerly looking forward to becoming a father. However, as time moved on and she didn't fall pregnant, I began to think there was something wrong with one or both of us. And that, unhappily, maybe clinical investigations would have to be . . . well, anyway, that Friday night, I found a blister pack of pills in a drawer. I asked her what they were for. She said they were vitamins and tried to snatch them back from me. I read the label and saw that they were contraceptives. I faced her with it. She admitted she had been taking them and I was furious. Essentially she said she wouldn't have her career jeopardized by becoming a mother at this time. We had the mother and father of all rows. We both yelled and she screamed a lot. She threatened to leave me. I said don't even think about it. I thought I had talked her round. I persuaded her to go away for a holiday, to think things over . . . gave her some money, a big cheque, to buy herself new clothes. It was a bribe really. I knew it was. Then, when she had gone, I busied myself getting the house how we wanted it. We had talked about the changes for months. I thought that when she came back it would please her, that it would make her happy and settle her down.'

He sighed as if he was glad to have told somebody.

'The rest, I think, you know.'

Angel thought a moment. He didn't want to be needlessly unkind.

'This throws a different light on matters, Mr Chancey. And being away so long, might she not have found someone else who—'

Chancey's eyes flashed. 'No. Never!' he bawled. 'She could *never* leave me!'

* * *

'Ahmed, I asked you to find DS Crisp for me. What the hell's going on?'

'I've tried everywhere, sir. I can't even raise him on his mobile.'

'Well, have another scoot round the station, leave a note on his desk or something, but find him. It's very urgent.'

The phone rang.

'Off you go.'

'Right, sir.'

Ahmed went out and closed the door, as Angel reached out for the phone.

'Angel.'

It was Edwin Larkin. He was phoning for his employer, Lord Tiverton. He passed the phone over to him.

'Tiverton here,' the old man growled. 'Look here. Have you made any progress in finding my suit of armour, Inspector?'

'We are doing our best, sir,' Angel replied lamely. 'Doing our very best.'

He knew it was not at all true, and he did hate lying but he couldn't tell the old man that he had a murder case on his hands and that it had a higher priority. He had circulated all the police forces, as well as the specialist national Art and Antiques section, but he hadn't had time to do anything else, there was such a lot happening.

'There are millions at stake, young man, millions! Last month my wife's diamond tiara was stolen from the jewellers. There went another three hundred thousand. It's outrageous, Inspector. Outrageous.'

'We are doing our best, sir,' Angel repeated. 'Please be assured of that.'

He could have told him that a tiara had been recovered, but as it had not been checked over by SOCO, nor identified as Tiverton's, he thought it might have been wrong to raise his hopes.

The old man didn't sound convinced; he growled and muttered something unintelligible, which ended in a few words that sounded like: 'the police were all flying bustards'.

'There's something else, Inspector,' Tiverton added. 'There's a wheelbarrow gone missing. Almost new, metal wheelbarrow. I ask you, what next? Put that down on the stolen list. It makes my blood boil. From now on, if I see any strangers mooching round here, I'll give them a blast of buckshot to remember me by, I'll tell you.'

There was a click and the line went dead.

Angel sighed. He was thinking that a thief might very well steal a wheelbarrow to transport a suit of armour away from the old carriage stables. It would be an ideal form of transport for it. Ergo, find a stolen wheelbarrow and you'll find a suit of armour. He must remember that.

There was a knock at the door. It was Crisp. Unusually, his cheeks were flushed and his eyes shining.

'There's a young woman in reception, sir. Her husband has left her, disappeared!'

Angel stared hard at him; his hands clenched tight. 'I don't do domestics, lad. You should know that by now. Just because a female member of the public, with a great pair of legs, comes in here—'

'Not only her legs, sir,' Crisp said pointedly with a smile.

'Comes in here with a sob-story, that her husband has left her, you're there, fawning all over her, trying to con her into going back to your flat for tea and sympathy and goodness knows what else.'

'*Sir*,' Crisp said protestingly.

'Oh, I forgot. You're engaged to WPC Leisha Baverstock, aren't you?'

Crisp looked away, his eyelids half-closed. 'No, sir. That's off. She gave me the . . . push.'

Angel's eyebrows shot up.

'Not surprised,' he said. 'And by the way, I am still awaiting a report from you about Peter Wolff.'

'There was nothing useful to say, sir.'

'Let me be the judge of that.'

'Well, I did the rounds. Spoke to over ten small-time hairdressers, you know, one person businesses, like most of them are, in Bromersley. Nobody knew him on a personal basis. They all really said that what he did wasn't the same type of business as they did. I can understand that. They looked after the middle-class ladies who could afford a mid-price maintenance job every week or fortnight or so, but the glamour girls, professional girls, women on TV or so who wanted a wig, at hundreds of pounds, that was Wolff's market.'

'What did you find out about his private life?'

Crisp shook his head. 'Wasn't married. Wasn't into crumpet, as far as I could find out, sir. Nothing.'

Angel rubbed a hand across his mouth, licked his lips quickly and said, 'You're not much of a detective, are you, lad?'

'If there *is* nothing, I can't make it up, sir,' Crisp said reasonably.

'All right. All right. Let's leave it at that for now,' Angel said, then added, 'And get rid of that woman in reception. But be gentle. Point her to the Salvation Army. They are good at missing persons. Or Relate or something. This just *isn't* the place.'

'But you haven't heard the interesting bit about her, sir.'

Angel's lips tightened back against his teeth. *'What, lad? What?'*

'She's the wife of Gabriel Grainger. The chap you put away for two years for tricking that woman out of her life savings. And she's asking to see *you*.'

Angel looked up. He remembered Gabriel Grainger. He drummed his fingers on the desktop, narrowed his eyes, then nodded. 'I remember him. His good looks were his downfall. Women of all ages just fell at his feet. He'll have been out of prison about a year now.'

He looked at the pile of post and bumf in front of him, rubbed his chin and said, 'All right. I'll have a quick word. Show her in, then nip off to Wolff's shop and see how SOCO are making out with that safe. We've got to stick with that case while it's still hot.'

'Right, sir.'

Crisp brought her down the corridor, showed her into Angel's office, closed the door and rushed off to Peter Wolff's shop.

The woman was dressed up to the nines, like a film star of the old school: long-sleeved summer dress, stockings, high-heeled shoes and carrying a black handbag.

'Thank you for seeing me, Inspector. My name's Zoe Grainger. I know you don't know me, but you knew my husband, Gabriel. I recognize you, because I was in court when he got sent down for two years.'

Angel liked the woman. She appeared to be straightforward and direct, and Crisp was right, she was very attractive; also her voice was deep and soothing, in contrast to the squawking nasal discord produced by skinny, American women infiltrating news programmes on British TV these days and copied by teenagers and others.

'Please sit down. Forgive me, Zoe. I don't remember you. If I had met you, I am sure I would have remembered.'

She smiled sweetly. It soon went.

'Gabriel and me weren't married then, Inspector. I was just a girlfriend then. One of many, I regret to say. I wish now, that that was how it had stayed, but I was soft and stupid. I married him three weeks after he came out of prison. Anyway, I'll get right to the point. I know you'll be busy. Trevor said that you don't normally see people reporting missing persons, because you get so many of them and that it isn't necessarily a crime.'

'That's true.'

'Well, I love my husband, Inspector. He's all I've got. And I want to do what I can to pull him out of whatever mess he might be in.'

'What mess is that?'

'Well, I don't know where to start. You see, Gabriel is easily led, Inspector. You might disagree on that point, but he is. After he was released he couldn't settle into a proper job. He had been a part-time model, but he lost interest in it. He's always been a bit of a philanderer. I knew that when I married him. I thought I could cure him of it, but . . . well, I haven't managed it yet. A pretty girl with a few quid and he was straight off the rails; he'd take her out, take her to bed, stay out late . . . 'til one or two in the morning. He'd come in drunk and . . . objectionable. This would last for a couple or three nights at the most. Then, he would get sick of her . . . and dump the poor cow, whoever she was. I've been living with this, tolerating it, but it hurts. Anyway, up to now he has always come back to me. And I've somehow got over it. Lived with it. Come to terms with it. In fact, we've had some really nice times. Not often, but we have. He can be a real charmer when he wants. But this time, Inspector, it's been thirteen days. Never been separated this long. Don't like being on my own without him. It'll be two weeks tomorrow. I don't know what's happened . . . haven't heard a word, not a single, damned word.'

She was close to tears, but she was also angry.

He nodded sympathetically. 'Please go on.'

'Well, on Friday night, the thirteenth . . . it must have been eight o'clock, he got a phone call. At first I thought it was one of his . . . women. He insisted it was a man offering him a job. For big money, he said. Very well-to-do, with great connections, he said. This is the opportunity I've been waiting for, Zoe, he said. Have faith in me, for once.'

She sighed. Then wrinkled her nose. It was a pretty nose.

'On reflection, on this occasion, I think it probably was a man,' she added. 'He rang again at about nine, to complete the arrangements.'

'He didn't give you his name?' Angel said.

'He said it was hush-hush and confidential. He told me that he had something afoot, a really important scheme that was going to pay off big time. He boasted that he was very well placed with somebody who was really going to put him on easy street, and that I wasn't to worry. He promised me that everything was going to be simply wonderful. All I had to do was trust him and believe in him. And he also said I'd never believe who it was. As if it was Donald Trump or somebody like that. Huh! He was such a practised liar. He once told me he was working for the CID. To tell the truth, I'd heard it all before! Anyway, he took some shirts, pyjamas and a razor and stuff in a suitcase, and said he didn't know how long he'd be away. I'll be back before you know it, he said. He left the house at about twenty past nine that night and I haven't seen or heard from him since. I'm afraid for his welfare, Inspector. I don't know what's going on. I am really afraid for him. Gabriel is arrogant, conceited, stupid and lovable. He isn't much, but he's my husband and I want him back.'

Angel sighed. 'Well, Zoe, you haven't given me much to go on, but I'll do my best.'

TEN

'Come in,' Angel called. The interruption disturbed his thoughts.

It was Gawber.

'What is it, Ron? I've just had Grainger's wife in here.'

'Yes. I saw her in reception. Nice-looking woman, too good for him.'

'Aye,' Angel enthusiastically agreed. 'What do you want?'

'You wanted a report on Katrina Chancey's credit cards.'

'Yes? Come in. Sit down.'

'Well, she had three. She certainly gave them some hammer. Her last transaction was Wednesday, the eleventh of April, two hundred and forty pounds at Monique's, a fashion shop in Leeds. Nothing since.'

Angel wrinkled up his nose. 'I wonder what she got for her money, a pair of matching handkerchiefs?'

'I've enquired, sir. It's on the chitty. She got a red dress. A Dare Devil model.'

A wry smile appeared for a moment. 'Magic,' he said. 'And what about her mobile?'

'Nothing since Friday the thirteenth. Just after four, she phoned the Top Notch model agency in London.'

'That it?'

He nodded.

Angel pursed his lips. 'She's disappeared and doesn't want to be found, or she's kidnapped, or — dread the thought — she's dead.'

Gawber sighed heavily.

'Gabriel Grainger left on Friday night, the thirteenth. Zoe's heard nothing since. The dates fit, Ron,' he said with a sniff.

'And he is known to be a hell of a philanderer.'

'Isn't it possible that they've pushed off together, sir?'

Angel sighed. 'Yes. Anything is possible. I don't know. But Grainger is an old customer, and I have a bit of an interest in him. We've got his pic in records. I want you to have it printed up — let Ahmed do it — and circulated round the station to all officers. He's been missing two weeks now. But that's a long time for a lump like that to be away from his wife, especially one as juicy as Zoe. Unless, of course, he prefers something younger with a barrel of money.'

Gawber smiled.

'I hope I am not going to have to be the one to tell her he's been found dead somewhere,' Angel added.

Gawber looked up. 'Why do you say that, sir?'

'Grainger's the sort of man who takes risks, unnecessary risks. Sometimes just for the hell of it. Just for the thrill of danger . . . he thinks the experience is worth more than the outcome. Zoe said that he was going on a job that offered big rewards. It required some travelling. He took a suitcase. Two weeks is a hell of a long time in this business, Ron. He could have travelled round the world in that time. We have to make of it what we can.'

Gawber couldn't make anything of it. He shook his head, went out and closed the door.

* * *

'Can't find DS Crisp anywhere, sir.'

'What?' Angel roared. 'Well keep looking. He should have been at Wolff's scene of crime. I'll have his skin when he does turn up.'

Ahmed stifled a smile. 'And there's DI Elliott to see you, sir.'

'Right, show him in, then buzz off and find Crisp.' Ahmed went. 'Come in, Matthew,' Angel called.

There were big smiles exchanged on both sides.

'Great to see you again. Sit down. Sit down.'

'I went straight to Wolff's shop,' Elliott said. 'Met your SOCO chap, Don Taylor. It's a great find, Michael. That safe is a treasure-trove in more ways than one. Taylor said there were prints on the plastic bags. Also some of the larger stones are big enough to have partial prints on them, so, with a bit of luck, he may be able to make an ID and give you a name or names. They may all be Wolff's own, of course. But you *might* get a useful lead.'

Angel's eyes shone briefly. There was the first possible lead to Wolff's murderer. His heart began to thump. A warm glow spread across his chest. 'That's good news, Matthew.'

Elliott smiled. 'Don Taylor says the cash total value is over four million pounds, almost all in twenty-pound notes.'

'The wig business was pretty good, eh?'

They smiled.

'Apart from a platinum diamond tiara, there is no finished jewellery. Wolff seemed to have been opening the settings, poking out the stones and sorting them into size and grade.'

'To obscure the source?'

'Almost certainly. And he seemed to know his stuff. He was mainly interested in large precious gemstones, diamonds, emeralds, rubies and sapphires. Each was kept separate and packed in a small polythene bag. The other stones, especially where they were small, under a carat or so, such as opals, turquoise, rhodolite (or red) garnets and so on were put in little polythene bags and then in boxes mixed. Large single stones, or specially interesting stones such green garnets or Mexican fire opals were separately bagged and boxed. There was very little gold or platinum there. Presumably he either melted the settings down himself to an amorphous lump, or sold the settings as they were, to a dodgy bullion dealer as scrap. There's plenty of them around.'

'I need to find the bullion dealer Wolff sold to.'

'Not easy.'

Angel rubbed his chin. 'There's usually at least one in every town.'

'Those chaps keep their dealings very private. They wouldn't even tell you whether it's raining or not.'

'And once the gold is melted, of course, there's no possible trace.'

'That's right. *And*, Michael, Wolff might have used a middleman. Extra security. Give a chap two per cent of a few thousand quid, a sort of handling charge. It can be a tidy figure, but a small expense to pay to obscure entirely his identity. He had plenty to worry about to make a thorough job of it. We, the police, may have been his first worry, but he also had predatory thieves, *and* the Inland Revenue to dodge.'

Angel nodded. 'Well, he was being very canny, separating the stones from the gold and platinum.'

'Exactly. He might have been equally canny in converting the gold, bullion and stones into cash.'

'Who would he sell the stones to?'

'There are specialist stone dealers in Hatton Garden. I'll ask around.'

'Right, Matthew. Thanks for coming so quickly. I'll wait to hear from you. I think I know where to start looking.'

* * *

Angel stopped his car outside Reuben's second-hand furniture shop on Doncaster Road. There was tatty furniture outside on the pavement in front of the window. There were six assorted chairs, a commode, and an old settee. They had price tickets made from scraps of cardboard stuck on to them with Sellotape. Behind them there were more handmade signs and placards stuck on the inside of the dirty shop window:

> 'Quality Furniture bought. Best prices paid.'
> 'House Clearances — same day.'
> 'Formica Table and two chairs £12.'
> 'Beds £12, £6 and £4.'
> 'Stag wardrobe with mirror £12.'
> 'Wedding rings bought.'
> 'Best prices paid for gold, silver and platinum.'

The inside of the shop was rammed jam-full of old furniture and household effects. The stuff was packed so tightly that a sort of tunnel had been created so that customers could squeeze through to reach the little kitchen in the back where the actual business was transacted.

The shop hadn't always looked like that. It used to be a bit smarter, when it was run by Frank Reuben, whose name was still across the window, but he was in Belmarsh for hijacking a van loaded with mint 20p pieces in South Wales in 2002. He had another year of his sentence to do.

For the time being, it was Dolly Reuben's business and she was running it her way.

Angel navigated his way through the short tunnel of dusty furniture, smelly upholstery and rolled up carpets. A bell rang as he stepped on to a piece of floorboarding, to forewarn Dolly of an approach.

He came through the arch and into the little room. There she was in a rocking-chair in front of the fire: a skinny, mean-looking woman with a big shock of red hair. She was smoking a cigarette and looking at the doorway expectantly as Angel came in. Standing by her with his back to the fire was her son and henchman, Timothy. It was hard to believe she was his mother. He was six feet two inches tall and must have weighed twenty-five stones. He had tattoos of a series of intertwined snakes up his arms. His eyes were dull and he usually looked down at the floor. He was lumpy, awkward and rarely spoke.

When Dolly Reuben recognized Angel, her face dropped and the chair stopped rocking. Without removing the cigarette from her mouth, she said, 'What do you want, Mr Angel?'

She had a voice like she gargled in petrol and could have stopped a Scottish pipe band with a single call.

Angel smiled. 'Just passing, Dolly. Just passing,' he lied.

She knew he was lying. It was just a game they played.

He looked round the tiny kitchen. There was nothing interesting . . . or illegal to observe. He knew there wouldn't be.

'Always nice to see you, Mr Angel.' Now she lied. 'Only used to seeing you when you're . . . a bit desperate . . . looking for something . . . that . . . that isn't there.'

He smiled again. 'Oh, it's there, all right, Dolly. It's just a question of putting your finger on it, you know?'

'You remember my son, Timothy?' she said, pointing a talon at the lump.

'Oh yes. How do, Timothy?'

The lump raised his head, nodded and then resumed gazing at the linoleum.

'Why don't you tell me what you're looking for and I'll tell you if I've seen it around.'

'Why not? Why not indeed? You may have known a man called Peter Wolff. He was a wig maker. Had a shop on Market Street.'

She shook her head.

He took out his wallet. In the fold he had three post-card-size photographs of Peter Wolff, Katrina Chancey and Gabriel Grainger. He fingered through them, selected the one he wanted and held it up for both of them to see.

'Timothy, we don't know this man, do we?'

The lump looked up, said, 'No Mam,' and resumed gazing at the linoleum.

'We don't know him, Inspector Angel,' she said with a sneer, which was the best she could manage for a smile. 'He's not been in *this* shop.'

'After he died we discovered a safe full of gemstones, gold, jewellery-parts and money.'

'Oh, really,' she croaked. 'Did you hear that, Timothy?'

'Yes, Mam.'

'Has he ever been in this shop, Timothy?'

'No, Mam.'

She nodded approvingly.

Angel sniffed and said, 'Turns out, he's the Fox, Dolly.'

'Really,' she said apparently uninterested. There was a silence, then she nodded and said, 'Feather in your cap then, eh, Inspector?'

114

'Sort of, I suppose, Dolly. Thing is, he was separating the stones from the settings, and selling the settings, presumably, as scrap.'

'Whatever next, Mr Angel?'

Angel rubbed his chin. 'Look, Dolly, I know you always say you don't know *anything* about anything that I ask you. On this occasion, a man was murdered. I know it wasn't pleasant going to court and seeing your Frank get sent down, but that was a case of robbery where nobody got hurt. Now this is very different. This is a case of murder. I'm not suggesting you had anything to do with it, but you wouldn't want to hinder my investigation into a murder case, would you?'

Dolly Reuben pulled a face like a stick of rhubarb and then shrugged.

'If you took in any of this man's scrap gold, and you had no reason to believe it had been acquired dishonestly, you have absolutely nothing to worry about.'

She took a heavy pull on the cigarette, blew a cloud in his general direction and then shook her head.

'If you know anything, for goodness' sake tell me. You may be able to tell me some small thing that might help me to find his murderer.'

'We don't know *nothing*, here, Mr Angel. I've told you.'

'Do you know, Dolly, there is an entire filing cabinet stuffed with papers and records that I haven't had time to look at. Peter Wolff, the Fox, was quite a meticulous keeper of records. If I later find out from some other source that you took any scrap gold or platinum in from him, I may charge you with hindering the police in the execution of their duty.'

'Push off, Mr Angel. I told you I don't know nothing, and you are hindering me in the execution of my work.'

His jaw muscles tightened. He put the photograph back into the fold of his wallet, pocketed it and took a step towards the way out, then he turned.

'That ancient settee you have out front, Dolly. Have you got a certificate to show that the stuffing is fire resistant?'

Her red eyes flashed. 'Eh? What? No.'

'Then you are committing an offence in offering it for sale. You'd better shift it off there, smartish. It's illegal to sell it.'

* * *

Angel banged the gear lever into first and pulled away from the front of Dolly Reuben's shop. She might be telling the truth, she might not. But either way, he wasn't going to be able to pierce that wall of denial. It came as no surprise that thieves trusted her with their stolen bullion. She must be a very rich woman.

This case was getting him down. There'd been no DNA, no fingerprints, no footprints, no witnesses, no sign of the weapon, and no motive. It was time for a lucky break. He was thinking he'd get Gawber and Crisp and Scrivens, if need be, to drop everything and concentrate on finding out where Wolff had sold his gold.

He turned the steering wheel of the BMW into the town centre and on to Victoria Street. Among the few pedestrians on the pavement he recognized a tall man in a smart raincoat, walking like a prince on an afternoon stroll. It was Irish John, John Corcoran to his friends. He wondered if he had anything for him.

Angel tapped down the indicator and pulled up to kerb. He lowered the car window.

'John,' he called. 'John!'

Irish John glanced back and then began to run.

Angel put the car in gear and began to drive alongside of him for forty yards or so, but he continued running.

Angel put his foot down, overtook him, stopped, got out of the car and stood by the car door.

'John,' he called. 'It's me!'

Corcoran saw him. His jaw dropped and he stopped running. He looked relieved and panted up to the car. 'Oh, it's you. For the loife of me, I tort you was the Costello brothers.'

'Get in,' Angel said. When they were both inside the car and had fastened their seatbelts, he said, 'Who are the Costello brothers?'

Corcoran shook his head.

'They're bad news,' he said. 'They're the reason I'm over here. I'd go back home if it wasn't for them. They run all the rackets in Dublin. If it makes money, they're into it.'

'What have you to do with them?'

'Nuttin'. Nuttin' at all. They say that I owe them money. Something to do with me going with one of their girls. I didn't know she worked for them else I would have dropped her like a hot King Edward's, I can tell you. I paid her and I bought her a lot of drinks. There are plenty of girls in Dublin since the liberation. I don't need to find a girlfriend out of Costello's clan. There's plenty of free enterprise. They reckon I owe them a service charge of a hundred euros. It's extortion, Inspector. Huh! Not likely.'

Angel turned into Church Street and across the front of Bromersley police station.

Corcoran's eyes flashed. 'Where are you taking me? I am not going in there! The rattle of handcuffs, the smell of all that blue serge and silver polish dries up me troat and brings out my rash.'

Angel smiled.

'All right,' he said. He changed up a gear, made three right turns and finished up in the car park of the Fat Duck.

Corcoran was all smiles.

They went inside. Angel ordered a Guinness and a bottle of German beer.

'I'm drinking this Guinness under false pretences, Inspector,' Corcoran said as he squatted down on a stool opposite Angel at a little table in the corner.

Angel couldn't pretend he wasn't disappointed. He wrinkled his nose.

'I asked around all the people I know,' Corcoran said. 'The people who I can trust. They'd all pretty much heard about the wig maker's murder, but there wasn't a whisper about the man's reputation . . . or anything else about him. None of them seemed to know him first hand. Well, none of my friends and acquaintances are in the business of wearing a wig, you'll understand, especially at his prices.'

Angel sighed, nodded resignedly and picked up his glass.

Corcoran said, 'I could easily have invented a tale about a mysterious witness, to oil the situation, but I am not as wicked as all that, not to a good friend like you, Inspector Angel.'

Nevertheless, Angel thought he must have told him some whoppers in his day. 'Thank you for trying, John.'

Corcoran nodded and sipped the black stuff.

They looked round the quiet bar. There were only two other men in the place.

Angel said, 'Did you get the chauffeuring job then, John?'

'No, sir. The suit was all right, but the hat didn't fit,' Corcoran said and returned to the Guinness.

Angel smiled. 'I'm sorry.'

'I'm not. The pay was rubbish. I was on the way to the Labour when you saw me.'

'Ah,' Angel said and put down the glass.

He was wondering whether he should give him a tenner or a twenty for his efforts, although he hadn't been of any use at all. He decided on a twenty. He liked the man, he wasn't grasping, he wasn't devious and he wasn't oily; he would almost certainly have spent the money issued to him on his release from HMP Boston.

Angel reached into his pocket and took out his wallet.

Corcoran's bushy eyebrows went up. 'Oh no, Inspector Angel, no handouts, please. I didn't find nuthin' out.'

'Treat it as a sort of . . . retainer,' Angel said.

Corcoran blinked. 'You're putting me on the books, loike?'

Angel nodded.

It seemed to satisfy Corcoran's scruples.

Angel opened the wallet on the table. The three photographs were still in the fold. The top one was Gabriel Grainger. The Irishman saw it. He pointed to it and smiled. 'Huh! Are you looking for *him*?'

Angel looked up. 'Do you know him?'

'I was on the same landing as him in the whole time I was in Armley in 2004,' he said.

Angel's jaw dropped.

'Ten long months. Poncy sort of chap. Always working out in the gymnasium he was. On exercise, he walked in the sun, if there was any. Never in the shade. He said he was trying to keep up a good skin colour.'

Angel's brain was playing snakes and ladders at the speed of broadband. 'Did you know him well? Did you know his name?' he said quickly.

He nodded. 'Graingerthestranger. I didn't know him well, but I knew him. He was one of the saner prisoners.'

'Yes. Yes. What else can you tell me about him?'

Corcoran frowned. 'Nuthin. You must want him for some-thin' big?'

Angel rubbed his chin. 'No, John. No. He's missing, that's all. His wife's worrying about him. As a matter of fact, he lives round here . . . in Bromersley.'

'Oh yes. I know'd that. I know'd that. Funny thing. I saw him about tree weeks ago.'

Angel's breathed in quickly. 'Where? Who with? When?'

Corcoran smiled. It was a rare occurrence. 'My goodness, he must be important. Whatever did *he* do?'

'He didn't do anything. But I'd like to find him. Where did you see him?'

'In the refreshment room at the railway station. He bought me a drink and the girl serving behind the counter. He bought me a bottle of Guinness and the girl a light ale, I remember. He had a wallet full of money. Flashed it about. Seemed he wanted everybody to see it. If he'd done that down some of the quayside pubs in Dublin he wouldn't have got far before he would have been relieved of it, I can tell you. Anyway, he certainly caught the eye of the serving girl, and after that, and a bit of mucky chat and sniggering, it was only the wooden counter that prevented them from having to pub- lish the banns to make it all legal. Talk about charm and good looks, Inspector. If anyone could have gotten Cherie Blair out of Number Ten any earlier, I reckon he could've done it.'

'You spoke to him?'

'Oh yes. He asked me when I had got out and I told him. He asked me about what job I had got and I told him I was still looking round. The rest of the conversation was more in the form of an address. He told me that he had a very posh job for a very wealthy person, and that he was going places . . . going up in the world. He was certainly well-turned-out.

Smart suit, raincoat and suitcase. And the job required him to travel away from home for the time being, everything paid for. Mindst you, he was talking partly for the benefit of the skirt behind the counter — boastful you know — who was lapping up all the honey he could make and hanging on his every word. It was wasted though, because his train came in and he had to leave her panting for more. However, she had to forget him when she was obliged to serve the neglected customers waiting patiently behind the counter for her attention.'

'And where was the train headed for?'

'Leeds, I tink . . . but *he* was going further, much further.'

'He could change at Leeds. You've no idea?'

'No.'

'And when was this?'

'Ah! Inspector Angel. I remember it well. The unluckiest day in the year, it was. *Friday, the thirteenth.*'

'Friday, the thirteenth . . . of April,' Angel said rubbing his chin.

'I remember that because I didn't want to go to my flat. It was unlucky. I was bound to be run over, or tumbled and my wallet stolen. Yet I knew the decision was imminent.'

'What time was this?'

'I don't know for certain. But it was late in the evening. I was in my cups and shortly afterwards, the young lady turned me out. She was closing the place, she was. She said she had to cash up and sweep the floor.'

Angel's mind began to buzz. There was something to think about. Maybe there was light at the end of the tunnel.

ELEVEN

The 16.02 train to Sheffield had just pulled out of Bromersley railway station leaving the platforms and the refreshment room deserted.

Angel pushed open the heavy brown door and saw a pretty young lady behind the counter. She was chewing gum and tidying up freshly washed teacups, saucers and glasses. He went straight over to her.

'Good afternoon, miss. Were you the young lady working here late on the evening of Friday, April the thirteenth?'

The girl stared at him warily as she lowered the wire tray of pots on to the counter. 'I might have been,' she said. 'Who wants to know?'

Angel pulled out his warrant card and badge and held it up for her. 'Police. Nothing to worry about. I'm interested in a man you served here that evening.'

She stopped chewing the gum and began to look interested. 'Oooh. That's two weeks back. There's only Mrs Mountjoy and me does evenings, and she was off then having her varicose veins stripped. Well, she's a lot older than me. It's these composite floors: hard as bell metal and cold as steel. April the thirteenth? Nearly three weeks ago? Yes. Mmmm. It would have been me. What man?'

He took out his wallet and showed her the photograph of Gabriel Grainger. It was a print of one originally taken in Belmarsh. It didn't particularly do him justice. She took it and stared sat it. She chewed the gum a couple of times, frowned, then eventually she smiled. 'Yes. Yeeees. That's the one. He was gorgeous.' Then her face changed. 'Crickey! Is he on the run?'

'No. He's gone missing. His wife is concerned. I'm trying to find him. That's all.'

She smiled. 'His wife? I bet she is. And with his money!'

Angel blew out a relaxed sigh. 'Do you happen to remember if he said where he was travelling to?'

She shook her head. 'He said he had an executive job with a very rich person. Travelled all over the place. I think he caught the ten twenty-eight to Leeds, but he was going on from there. I close at ten-thirty. I remember he left before I shot the bolts. He was lovely, though. A real hunk.'

'Did he have any luggage?'

'Brown leather suitcase, I think.'

'But you don't know where he was headed?'

'Sorry,' she said. 'But wherever it was, I wish I'd gone with him,' she added, then returned to chewing the gum.

* * *

'It may be just a coincidence, sir,' Gawber said.

Angel glared at him across the desk, his lips tightened against his teeth. 'Ron,' he said. 'How many times do I have to tell you that in the murder business, there's no such thing as coincidence?'

123

Gawber's eyebrows went up. Angel was always saying that.

Angel ran his hand through his hair. 'I have drawn a complete blank trying to find out where Grainger was travelling to on that Friday night, the thirteenth. His wife says that he left his house with a suitcase at approximately nine-twenty. At nine-thirty, he arrived at the waiting room in Bromersley station with a wallet full of money, which he must have been given or picked up at some point. He booked a ticket to somewhere — thought to be to Leeds — then disappeared. Eight hours later, Katrina Chancey is supposed to have left her home by some transport we have not been able to trace, to who knows where? Nothing heard of *her* since.'

'From that, sir, what do you deduce?'

'I don't know, Ron. It's obvious that they might have met up somewhere, but Zoe Grainger says that it was a man's voice on the phone telling her husband where to meet and at what time. If it had been some straightforward mucky weekend between two adults there would not have been a male voice directing him, would there? It would simply be a double adultery . . . sadly, happening all the time, but it's not a police matter. Also, it wouldn't have been Chancey's voice on the phone. He's not likely to be engineering an arrangement for Grainger to run off with his wife and have given him some cash to pay for the wherewithal to enjoy themselves.'

Gawber nodded. He agreed. He rubbed his chin.

'Who else is there, sir?'

'Zoe Grainger said it was definitely a man.'

After a moment, Angel said, 'If they met, what reasons, apart from the obvious, would they have met for?'

Gawber looked up and said, 'You don't think Grainger, with or without the collusion of Katrina Chancey, is setting up a blackmailing situation to extract money from Frank Chancey, do you?'

'I don't know, Ron. Why would a woman enjoying a great career as a model and happily married to a multimillionaire, a handsome multimillionaire at that, bother with a poverty-stricken, ex-con loser like Grainger? All right. He's a great-looking bloke. A furtive, dirty little weekend might be tempting, . . . stretched out to a week, but not *three* weeks, and it would be difficult to believe that she was contemplating a long-term commitment. Also, she was supposed to be a mad, mad career woman. Doing well both sides of the Atlantic. Was she willing simply to dump it without telling her agent? Nobody actually saw Katrina leave the house. You and Trevor Crisp could not find the taxi, specialist holiday hire car outfit, friend, relation or anybody to actually admit to collecting her and taking her anywhere. Nor did any member of her staff. And Frank Chancey had already left for the office. He didn't take her to the airport either. And her own car was still in the garage.'

'All this happened three weeks ago, tomorrow. And we have not seen or heard a word. Don't you realize, sir, they could both be dead?'

Angel shuddered briefly and looked disapprovingly at him. 'Give up, Ron. Don't be so pessimistic. Of course, that possibility has gone through my mind. But I've known people be missing for a lot longer than three weeks and still turn up as fresh as . . . as Mary Archer.'

Gawber nodded. It was true.

Angel sighed. Then, 'I am sick of this,' he suddenly called out. 'If it wasn't for the super I wouldn't be consuming valuable time on this Chancey business at all. I should be giving my full attention to finding the murderer of Peter Wolff. I don't want that case going cold on me. But I am stuck on that one, Ron, I must confess. There are some pieces missing. Or there is something I cannot yet see.' He frowned, sighed, shook his head and said, 'I feel like a blind man in a darkened room looking for a black cat that isn't there.'

Gawber smiled to himself. Despite what he had said, his boss thrived when he was under pressure and had several cases to deal with simultaneously. He had seen the great man working on three entirely separate cases at the same time, carrying the multifarious strands of each case in his memory. He had seen him do it. For Angel it was a challenge and he loved it. He had seen him absorb the facts, then weigh the probabilities, the improbabilities, the uncertainties and the likelihoods, and then, 'hey presto!' out popped the identity of the guilty party and a full explanation as to how the crime had been executed. Angel seemed to be able to apply all the permutations to the situation and eventually arrive at the one and only result that fitted all the facts. In time, he had always managed to solve the unsolvable, and Gawber had every faith that he would manage to find Wolff's murderer and the whereabouts of Katrina Chancey and Gabriel Grainger very soon.

* * *

It was Flat 4. Angel knocked on the door. It was some time before there was any response and then the door was quickly yanked opened and a bright-eyed Zoe Grainger appeared.

'Oh, it's you, Inspector,' she said, panting. She put her hand to her chest. 'Have you brought me some news . . . of my husband?'

He licked his lips. 'I'm sorry, no.'

She pulled the door open wider. 'Come in.'

'Just a few questions, Zoe,' he said. 'I hope I'm not calling at an inconvenient time?'

'No. Not at all,' she said, closing the door. 'Have you no idea where he might have disappeared to? It's three weeks today. When you knocked just now I just thought that . . . I hoped it might be him. That he might have lost his key, or . . .'

'Sorry to have raised your hopes.'

'Please sit down. I am getting to think the worst, Inspector. I really am. Questions?'

'Yes. On the night he went, you said that there were two phone calls, and that your husband answered both.'

'Yes. They were both for him. The first one he took upstairs on the bedroom extension, and the second down here about ten minutes later.'

'You did not speak to the caller or overhear your husband's side of the first call?'

'No, I didn't.'

'What did you overhear of the second call? It is vitally important to tell me everything you know.'

'I couldn't hear what was actually being said by the caller, of course, but the voice sounded loud, deep and sort of urgent.'

'Was the caller a man?'

'It was definitely a man. From what my husband said, as near as I can remember, he was to pack a bag, meet him or somebody in ten minutes. He was going away. He didn't know where to or for how long. Last words were, "there's money in this, Zoe. Big money. Have faith in me. Trust me. I'll be back before you know it". I said I didn't believe him, that I'd trusted him before and that he was a born liar. And some other dreadful things I wished I hadn't. I didn't know then what he was up to. Still don't.'

'When he left, did he have much money on him?'

'He couldn't have had more than ten pounds, from his unemployment money, that I know.'

'He was seen in the refreshment room at Bromersley railway station shortly after he left here brandishing a wallet full of twenty-pound notes.'

Her jaw stuck out and her bottom lip quivered. 'Must have got it from one of his women,' she said. 'Was he with a woman?' she added quickly. 'I bet he was with a woman.'

'No, he wasn't, actually. Witnesses say that he was alone.'

She raised her head. 'What was he doing at the railway station, Inspector?'

'He caught a train, we believe to Leeds. Does he have any particular friend in Leeds? Or anywhere else, for that matter?'

'I told you, he has women all over the place. I can't think of any one of them he'd want to be with for three weeks. After a few days he always came back to me,' she said looking down.

Angel wrinkled his nose, rubbed his chin, then said, 'You or your husband don't happen to know a woman called Katrina, do you? She's a model, I believe.'

Zoe's head came up. Her eyes flashed. 'Is he with her? Is there something you're not telling me?'

'No. Not at all. It's just that . . . she also seems to be missing.'

'I know her. Local girl. Seen her in loads of magazines and TV ads. I've seen him ogling her in the underwear section of Grattan's catalogue. She's very young. In her teens.'

'She's twenty-two. Went missing on Saturday morning, the fourteenth of April, the morning after.'

Her pretty mouth tightened. 'He likes the young ones.'

Angel sniffed. 'The thing is, Zoe, did he know her?'

'I don't know who he knows, Inspector. Where did she go missing from?'

'From her house. She's married. Lives on Creesforth Drive off Creesforth Road.'

'Mmm. My Gabriel likes them rich, as well. He *may* have known her. We don't normally mix in such elevated circles, but he was never backward at coming forward. What's her husband say?'

* * *

Harker raised his ginger eyebrows. 'Thirty-six pairs of shoes of varying sizes?'

'Yes, sir.'

'What's the point of that? Were they for different women?'

'No, sir. That's the point. Chancey ordered from the store. He selected them himself. Chose each pair. To restock his wife's wardrobe, he said. He had thrown her other shoes away.'

'Well,' Harker growled. 'Have you asked him why?'

'You wanted me to treat him with kid gloves. What excuse could I possibly make to question him? It would be akin to asking him if he had gone round the twist. And he wouldn't take kindly to being considered a murder suspect . . . friend of the chief constable and all that. Now, I want permission to treat Chancey in the ordinary way. There might be a perfectly innocent explanation as to why he would buy his wife shoes in different sizes. I can't think of one, but there might be. Maybe he's got the hots for the girl in the shoe shop, and she's on commission? I don't know, but to me, it smells fishy. His wife going missing like that, things might not be what they seem. I need to seize all his footwear to check for precious metal dust, gold, platinum, whatever. Just to eliminate him.'

Harker pursed his lips. 'No. No. Can't do that. Not without specific permission.'

There was a pause. Angel looked across at Harker.

'Will you get me that permission, sir?' he said, nodding at the phone.

'He's in Bournemouth at a conference. Can't interrupt him for that, lad.'

* * *

Angel turned the bonnet of the BMW through the open gates of Chancey House, down the drive, through the bushes to the front of the house. The first thing that met his eye was the spray of water from the mouth of the statue of a water baby or whatever it was, reaching over eight feet high from the huge marble fountain in front of the main entrance to the house. He gazed at it for a few seconds. It was truly magnificent. With the foundations, the marble figure and surround must weigh ten tons or more. It must surely impress Katrina Chancey and make her count her blessings and reflect upon her husband's great wealth when she returned. If she ever did return.

Behind him came the SOCO van with DS Taylor driving it. He parked it next to the BMW and joined Angel at the main entrance as he rang the bell.

Shortly it was answered by Mrs Symington.

'Hello, Inspector. Did you want to see Mr Chancey? He's at the office, you know. Not expected back until much later this afternoon.'

Angel feigned surprise. 'Oh? It's about having all Mr Chancey's footwear checked over. Is it not convenient?'

Mrs Symington frowned and blinked several times.

He looked at Taylor. 'We've made a fruitless journey, Sergeant. It's Friday. You won't be able to get back until Monday at the earliest, will you?'

'No, sir. Be three weeks at least, sir. The equipment has to go back.'

Angel nodded. 'Oh yes. Pity. A lot can happen in that time.'

Taylor shook his head and looked down.

Mrs Symington said, 'What exactly do you want? What are you talking about?'

'It's a matter of hygiene,' Angel said. 'Radio activity and gamma rays.'

'And computer viruses,' Taylor added.

Mrs Symington's jaw dropped open.

'Cleanliness is next to godliness,' Taylor said.

'So easy to pick up on one's shoes,' Angel said. 'I was going to check over Mr Chancey's footwear to check that he wasn't carrying any of those in the form of computer spam around and infecting the house and the carpets.'

Taylor said, 'It's so easily picked up in the dirty streets, factories, offices and places.'

'DS Taylor has the equipment here in the van,' Angel added.

Mrs Symington looked him up and down. 'There's no infection in the carpets, here, Inspector. They have all just been dry-cleaned.'

'I know, and he wants to keep them like that,' Angel said. 'And I don't blame him. He wants everything to *stay* spotless.'

'You can't *see* it, you see, Ma'am. Like BSE, mad cow disease.'

Angel glanced at Taylor. He thought that might have gone too far.

Mrs Symington frowned.

There was a pause.

Angel said, 'If you think Mr Chancey would be happy to wait a month or whenever . . . ?'

'No. No,' she said. 'What exactly needs to be done, Inspector?'

Angel and Taylor exchanged glances.

Angel explained that he needed all Mr Chancey's footwear for checking and that the whole business would take ten or fifteen minutes only at the most.

Mrs Symington quickly disappeared and returned to the door a few minutes later with three large plastic bags containing twelve pairs of shoes, three pairs of slippers, a pair of flip flops, two pairs of tennis shoes and a pair of deck shoes.

Angel eagerly took them from her, went round to the back of the SOCO van and handed them up to Taylor who was inside, now wearing white paper overalls and thick rubber gloves.

Angel climbed in and sat on a fitted hinged seat opposite him, hoping for a positive result.

Taylor wiped the sole of each shoe separately with methylated spirit to remove any oil or grease; then dipped a one-inch brush into a glass jar, which contained a dangerous liquid comprising a concentration of two parts of hydrochloric acid to one-part nitric acid, with a thimbleful of potassium nitrate. He quickly applied a thin coat of the highly corrosive stuff to the sole of the shoe, carefully avoiding any destructive splashing. After each application he examined the shoe sole closely. In the presence of any gold and platinum and palladium dust, there would have been an instant bubbling in response to acid working on metal. The bubbling would have been in a colour that would have indicated the particular precious metal and its purity. There was no reaction at all, so there was no metal present. The shoe sole was instantly doused in water and wiped dry, to stop the acid continuing to act and eat into the leather.

Taylor was not having any luck. He applied a coat of the acid on to the last shoe and held it up to the light. A wisp of white vapour drifted upwards, but there was no other reaction from the sole. That was it. There had been no sign of a precious metal on any of Chancey's shoes. He quickly doused the last shoe in cold water, wiped it vigorously with cotton waste and passed it to Angel.

'That's it, sir. Nothing.'

Angel was disappointed. He sighed loudly. His belly felt as hollow as a conman's promise. He had thought it possible that Chancey was the murderer of Peter Wolff. The nonsense of the shoes of different sizes for Katrina somehow triggered something subconsciously in Angel's mind. But he must have been wrong. Chancey didn't have a motive. It had not been a good idea. It could not have been him.

'Could be the pair of shoes he's wearing now,' Taylor said as sort of consolation.

'Could be,' Angel said. But he didn't really think so. He agreed though, that as a matter of proper scientific thoroughness they should be checked.

He put the last shoe into the plastic bag, alighted from the SOCO van, crossed to the house entrance and rang the doorbell.

Mrs Symington appeared.

He forced a smile as he handed her the bags of shoes.

'Were they all right?' she asked.

'Absolutely perfect clean,' Angel said. 'Nothing to worry about there, Mrs Symington.'

'Thank you, Inspector,' she said, beaming.

'It's a pleasure,' he lied.

The door closed.

He turned. He was facing the new fountain. He gazed at it again for a few seconds. It was truly magnificent. With the foundations, it must weigh ten tons or more.

Princess Diana had a water feature built in her memory he recalled.

He wondered where Katrina Chancey was . . . whether she was alive or dead. If she was dead, where was she buried?

TWELVE

It was Saturday, 5 May.

The sun was shining. Birds were singing. Rottweilers were barking. It was the first day of the weekend. The day Angel would normally have looked forward to. It should also have been a welcome relief from the tedious job of searching for the murderer of Peter Wolff, an investigation with nothing to go on and for which, as yet, there seemed to be no motive. It should have been respite from the peculiar business of looking into the disappearance of missing glamour girl Katrina Chancey, whose husband was a friend of the chief's, and all the complications that that had made, and searching for missing glamour-boy, mister handsome himself, Gabriel Grainger, every housewife's comforter and friend. The last two, he accepted, might simply be missing persons, who could be ensconced somewhere, together or separately, safe and happy as pigs in the proverbial. He didn't know that for certain. He knew nothing for certain. Everything led to a dead end. He had spent all week hard at it and made little progress.

It should have been a day of rest and relaxation, but he had promised to take Mary to Harrogate to collect the Chippendale table, for which she had paid £500. He had made the promise reluctantly and under duress, but a promise is a promise. And Mary always got her own way.

They had an early lunch and Mary had pulled out some dust sheets, old sheets and blankets to wrap the table in to protect it from further damage on the journey back. From her description, Angel thought that it would fit satisfactorily in the closed boot of the car and so off they went.

He had driven the BMW through Harrogate on the Ripon road and Mary was directing him. There were some complex twists and turns before they reached the leafy country lane with more potholes than needle-marks on a junkie's arm. The gates to Mr Seymour Timms's house and garden were open, so Angel drove straight in and up to the house. His heart sank when he saw the neglected state of the fence, the gates, the house and greenhouse.

'What a dump,' he said.

'It's all right. It's all right. It doesn't matter to him. All he's interested in his chrysanthemums,' Mary explained.

She got out of the car. 'Come on. Can you see him anywhere?'

Angel muttered something unhelpful, got out of the car and locked the door with the remote. There was no sign of life. He looked round. And then suddenly through the gap in the bushes, he saw the huge show of bright colours reflecting the bright May sun. It was a strikingly colourful display of row upon row of chrysanthemums. It lightened his heart. He took in the colours and the smell. Even from that distance. He stood there with a smile on his face. The first proper relaxed smile since he'd heard that the Met had arrested two of the men wanted in connection with the London bomb plot. He breathed deeply. Then, from where he stood, he swivelled around the entire 360° to survey the site to find the whereabouts of Seymour Timms.

'Where is the old codger, then?'

An elderly voice behind them said, 'Good afternoon, I suppose I must be the old codger, sir.' He said dryly, then he doffed his hat and replaced it. 'Seymour Timms is what most people call me,' he added with a smile. 'What can I do for you?'

He must have dodged out of one of the greenhouses behind them and they had not noticed.

Mary looked surprised. 'It's Mrs Angel, Mr Timms. I bought that table from you.'

His pale face brightened. 'Ah yes, of course.'

'And this is my husband.'

'Pleased to meet you, sir. You've come to collect it. Of course. Of course. It is assembled the best way it could be by the carpenter . . . behind the conservatory. Come this way. But first, you must come and see what the carpenter has done for me.'

They followed Timms towards the conservatory, tacked on to the nearest side of the tumblety house. The door was wide open and he put an arm out to show a number of shelves of different heights from the top to the bottom, with a large table surface below, all in new unpainted timber. Mary could see that he had more than twice as many pots there now and she also noticed the blue-and-white Wedgewood bowl placed in the familiar position on the corner nearest the door.

'Your brilliant idea,' Timms said with a smile, looking at Mary. 'I was very worried at first, but the local carpenter turned out to be first class. He fitted me shelves just how and where I needed them and I got a little bit of change out of the cheque you paid me for the table. So I hope everybody is happy.'

Mary smiled. 'I'm very happy, Mr Timms, thank you.'

Angel looked at her and frowned.

Timms went round the back of the conservatory to the far side. They followed behind.

'Here's your table, Mrs Angel. I put the hose on it . . . removed most of the earth off it before I got the carpenter to set it up here.'

As they followed Timms, Mary grabbed her husband by the arm and whispered in his ear, 'Look, Michael, it's old, it's antique and it's made by Thomas Chippendale. You may not think much to it, but it's a work of art, it's a bargain and I've bought it with my own money.'

Angel looked at her and frowned.

'So I don't want you making a scene,' she added. 'All right?'

He shrugged.

Then he saw it. He stared at it dumbstruck.

It was a plain straightforward table, four feet long by two feet deep, with a heavily scratched top set on three tapered legs. At the corner where the fourth leg should have been it was propped up with a pile of thick, musty and very old books.

'Thank you very much, Mr Timms,' Mary said with a big smile.

Angel gasped. 'There's a leg missing,' he grunted. 'Where is it? A table's no good with a missing leg. I mean to say . . .'

Mary glared at him with a face like a judge with piles. 'Leave it, Michael. I said, leave it. I bought it with three legs, as it is. The deal is done. Will you put it in the car, Michael, please?'

'Can I assist with the loading, dear lady?' Timms said touching his hat.

'You must be off your head,' Angel muttered. 'I knew there was some insanity in your family. Your mother was never right . . . she went a bit funny in the end. It's in the genes—'

Her face was scarlet. 'Will you shut up and put it in the boot?'

He picked up the table from the column of books and carried it easily the twenty yards or so to the car, shaking his head and muttering all the while. He wrapped it, pointlessly he thought, in the sheets she had brought and lowered it easily into the car boot.

Mary followed behind him angrily, stamping her shoe heels into the ground.

Timms followed a few moments later with the books in a wheelbarrow.

Angel looked at the old man strangely as he packed them into the boot. He then looked at Mary who sniffed and stuck her nose in the air.

When the wheelbarrow was empty Angel closed the boot and, without a word, unlocked the car doors. He got into the driver's seat and put on his seat belt.

Timms and Mary shook hands, said their goodbyes, then she got into the car.

Angel started the engine, turned the car round to face the gate. The last Angel saw of Seymour Timms was in his rear-view mirror. The old man was trudging towards the greenhouses, pushing the wheelbarrow.

There was a difficult silence in the car all the way home. In fact, there was almost total silence in the Angel house the entire weekend.

* * *

It was 8.28 a.m., Monday, 7 May. Angel drove the BMW determinedly along Creesforth Road, down Creesforth Drive then left through the open gates of Chancey House, and along the drive up to the magnificent fountain in the gravel square at the front entrance of the great house. He got out of the car and turned to look at and listen to the water display. Water spewed in a beautiful form out of the mouth of the cupid character on a pedestal in the centre of the big round marble edging that formed the wall, which contained the water. He walked up to the edge and looked downwards into it. It was about two feet deep. The sound of it shooting up then trickling down was pleasant, repetitive, almost hypnotic.

It certainly made the entrance to Chancey House most imposing.

Katrina Chancey would surely be impressed, if she was ever coming back to see it . . . wherever she was.

He meandered round the perimeter of the fountain rubbing his chin. He wondered where Katrina Chancey was at that moment . . . even if she was alive. Although a lot of searching and enquiries had been made, it had not actually been possible to determine that she had ever left the house for Rome that Saturday morning. There were positively no witnesses of it. They had enquired everywhere. He intended going through Frank Chancey's evidence again. There must be something he had overlooked or perhaps there was something he simply wasn't revealing.

He turned away from the fountain towards the main entrance to the house when he heard a mobile phone very faintly. He reached into his pocket automatically, although he knew it wasn't his ring tone. No, it wasn't his phone. He looked around. It was very faint and was near the fountain. He walked up to the fountain to try to home in on the sound.

He thought it came from the middle of the fountain, if that was possible. Then, as abruptly as it started, it stopped.

His narrowed his eyes. Had he really heard the ring of a mobile phone coming from the centre of the fountain, so early on a May morning? It was hard to believe. There was nobody else around. And then a horrific thought crossed his mind.

At that same moment, the handsome figure of Frank Chancey appeared at the entrance of the house. His eyebrows shot up when he saw Angel hovering over the fountain.

'What brings you to admire my lovely fountain at this early hour, Inspector?'

'Good morning, Mr Chancey. Strange thing, you know. I just heard a mobile phone ring. It came from underneath the fountain.'

'What?' Chaney said with a smile. 'It must have been the birds, old chap. It is the beginning of May, you know.'

A burgundy Rolls Royce drove up from behind the house to the front entrance and stopped.

'I wanted to have a word with you, sir,' Angel said.

'Sorry. Not just now. Appointments all morning. Give my secretary a ring.'

The chauffeur wore a nebbed hat. He looked in Angel's direction and waved. Angel recognized him. It was Lyle. He acknowledged the wave.

'Must go. Excuse me,' Chancey said. He stepped into the limousine, the car pulled away and was on its way up the drive while Angel stood there rubbing his chin.

Angel stared at the fountain, his ears straining to hear the mobile phone ring tone again. He stood in front of it listening to the fall of the water for ten minutes or more, then he turned away. He meandered round the fountain one more time, then he suddenly stuck his hand into his jacket pocket for his own mobile. He opened it and dialled a number.

'Ahmed, I want you to look in the file on my side table, labelled Katrina Chancey. I want her mobile phone number.'

Two minutes later, he was tapping out the number on his mobile. He pressed the send button and waited expectantly by the fountain.

The sound of a mobile phone rang out again. His pulse raced. He could hear it faintly. There was no doubt about it. It seemed to come from under the centre of the statue. It definitely emanated from Katrina Chancey's missing mobile! How had it got there? The question had to be asked: was the body of the missing woman underneath the fountain also?

* * *

By 11 a.m. that morning the fountain had been drained dry, the marble slabs and the central pedestal figure removed and piled on a neat heap close by.

Angel had notified the police workshops at Wetherby and they had sent a heat-seeking camera team of two men, who were working over the central area of the fountain base. They were trying to trace heat that was naturally generated by the chemical disintegration of a dead body. Sophisticated machines can register heat changes to a fine degree through six feet of soil, and even after several months, sometimes years.

The DS had been panning the area with the heat detector, which was rather like a metal detector, but with a span area of about the size of a dustbin lid, for around ten minutes. He suddenly stopped, switched off the machine, looked up at the DI and shook his head.

Angel was standing by his car, hands in his pockets trying to look like Fred Astaire waiting for the music to start. He'd given up smoking four years ago, but this was a time when he would gladly have given fifty quid for a drag.

The DI in charge of the team came across to Angel, shaking his head.

He knew it was bad news. They hadn't found a body. They hadn't found anything.

'The waterpipe and plumbing we can work round, Michael, but it's the concrete base. It must be well over six inches thick. We can't get a reading through it. Sorry.'

The DS began loading the machine in the little blue van.

Angel's face tightened. 'Oh,' he sighed. 'Thanks for turning out promptly. The concrete is over eighteen inches thick. I know, I saw them pouring it.'

The DI nodded. 'I'll get our road gang down this afternoon, if they're available,' he said, rapidly tapping numbers into his mobile. 'Two hydraulic drills should shift that in three or four hours. If not they'll come tomorrow morning. Don't worry, Michael, if there's a body down there, we'll find it.'

Angel sighed again and chewed on air.

'See you about one-thirty, or I'll give you a ring,' he said and they drove the little blue van away on the exit road.

Angel watched them go, then turned and made for his car.

As the van disappeared through the bushes on the 'out' road, the burgundy Rolls Royce appeared on the 'in' road, coming quickly towards him. Almost before it stopped, Frank Chancey bounced out of it, red-faced and waving his arms in the air.

'What the hell is going on!' he screamed. 'What have you done to my fountain?'

Angel took in a deep breath. 'I have reason to believe that the body of your wife is in the foundations. So I am naturally—'

'Ridiculous. Absolutely ridiculous. She's not dead. Nobody's dead. She has left me. It's hard for me to admit, Angel. Very hard for me to admit. A man of my standing and position in society, but she has gone. The woman who had everything has left the man who has everything. She's not right in the head. If she had intended returning she would have turned up by now, but she has not. I am trying to come to terms with it. It is difficult. But there was no need to take the fountain to pieces. It cost over eighty thousand pounds. I don't know what it's worth now. Look at it. Just look at it. I am not standing for it. I shall charge you whatever it costs to bring it back to how it was. Vandalism, it is. Absolutely vandalism. I'll speak to the chief constable about all this, Angel. It's outrageous!'

Lyle got out of the Rolls Royce, locked the door and stood behind Chancey, looking everywhere except at either of the two men.

'You must do whatever you think, sir,' Angel said. 'I told you I heard a mobile phone ringing out under the fountain. I discovered that it was your wife's, so it suggested to me that your wife's body might also be there. You presumably have not heard from her for over three weeks now, and her model agency has heard nothing, her bank account and mobile phone accounts have not been used. I have every reason to believe that she is dead, perhaps murdered, and that she is buried under there,' he said pointing at the big concrete base.

'She isn't there, you stupid flatfoot,' Chancey said. His face was redder than a judge's robe. 'She's changed her identity, hasn't she? She's found somebody else. How many times do I have to tell you? She's gone. Vamoosed. You didn't have to cause all this mess. This vandalism will cost you your job!'

The muscles on Angel's face tightened. His heart beat harder than the drummer in the police pipe band. 'I was given the job of searching for her, sir. I intend to try and finish the job.'

'We will see,' Chancey said. He flounced through the main entrance into the house, followed by Lyle, who seemed to have taken an unusual interest in the ground and walls of the house.

Angel sniffed, turned and looked at where the fountain had been.

* * *

It was four hours later. The area around the fountain base was crowded with vehicles. There were two Range Rovers with compressors on trailers behind them, with connections to hydraulic drills being held by men working on the concrete base. They were systematically cutting into the perimeter, working towards the centre; there were two other men clearing away the broken-down concrete and soil; there was the DI from Wetherby, in charge of the excavation unit, DS Taylor and DI Angel and their respective vehicles. Angel and Taylor were standing on the perimeter of the foundations, keenly watching the concrete as the pieces were chipped off the main block, dreading what might be revealed as each shovelful of concrete and soil was removed.

Angel suddenly spotted the shiny grey case of the mobile phone. The skin on the back of his hands and arms turned to gooseflesh. The mobile was revealed in wet earth underneath a freshly broken chip of concrete. It appeared to be in good condition.

'There!' he yelled over the deafening hammer of the hydraulic drills and hardworking compressors. 'The phone!

There!' he yelled, gesticulating wildly. He didn't want the drill to shatter through the case and ruin any of the precious information it might be able to provide. The PC saw it, took his hands off the trigger of the drill, leaned forward and with a gloved hand picked it out of the sludge. DS Taylor opened up an EVIDENCE bag, and the PC dropped the mobile straight into it. The DS then rushed off in a marked police car back to the station to begin the tests. He could check the phone for any prints that might show the last person to handle it and who might have dropped it into the foundations of the fountain, also the recent call history. It was potentially brimful of useful information.

Angel nodded with satisfaction at the find. It could prove to be invaluable in providing evidence. He also had the pleasure of knowing he had not gone completely bananas. Its presence showed that he had actually heard the phone ring. He *had* heard the mobile ring out.

The DI from Wetherby together with Angel stood on the perimeter of the foundations, expecting any second to see a hand, an arm or a foot appear beneath a freshly cut piece of concrete or shovelful of brown soil.

For another hour, the drills kept drilling, the concrete kept breaking away into small pieces, the shovellers kept shovelling, but even when they had completely broken down the slab, cleared it, and applied the heat detector to the soil beneath, there was no corpse there, nor had there ever been.

THIRTEEN

It was 8.28 on Tuesday morning.

It was no surprise to Angel to be summoned up to Harker's office, first thing, after the frustrating business of the day before.

Angel was surprised that Harker hadn't phoned him at home the previous evening. He was bound to have had an earful from the chief constable about him. Chancey was bound to have griped to the chief, with whom he would have been drinking in the Feathers, the golf club, or the Masonic or wherever they go to massage each other's egos, and he would have inevitably passed it on to Harker.

He knocked on the door.

'Come in!' Harker bawled. 'Come in. Sit down.'

Angel looked across the desk at him. He looked as unpleasant as a body at an exhumation. His complexion was like putty and his nose was like a Victorian bath tap. The smell of TCP was sickly.

Angel sat down and said nothing.

Harker leaned forward over his desk and spoke in an icy voice as though he was auditioning for the part of Himmler.

'I don't know what to say to you. I think you might have gone off your chump. I told you distinctly to make gentle enquiries about a missing wife. Nothing more. I didn't expect you to knock down the husband's marble fountain costing eighty thousand pounds simply to retrieve her mobile.'

'Her mobile might be very valuable to us, sir. But, also, I thought she was under there. I heard the phone ring out. I checked it was her number. It was, so I put two and two together.'

'The two and two, is that all you had to go on to assume she was dead?'

'No sir. Three weeks have passed, and nothing has been heard of her. No movement on her credit cards, her bank account or her telephone.'

'You know that's simply not enough, these days. Looks as if she simply doesn't want to be found. She's a very rich and talented young woman in her own right. Anyway, you were not instructed to take this matter any further than to find the woman. You were not instructed to treat it as a fully blown murder investigation.'

Angel wasn't getting as much stick as he had expected. He was surprised. He was also a bit annoyed. He was always getting told off for doing what was really the obvious and intelligent thing to do. When it didn't work out right, he got a rocket. He wasn't gifted with hindsight.

He thought that the best means of defence was attack, so he decided to take a chance. He wrinkled his nose and said, 'Well, sir, are you taking me off this case, because of the fact that the chief constable and Chancey are friends, or do you want me to continue with my investigation to find the murderer?'

That disturbed Harker's equilibrium. Angel hoped it would, but he mustn't go too far.

Harker's eyes flashed a moment, then returned to normal. He didn't answer for a few moments, then icily, he said, 'Just because you have had a few little plaudits in connection with your investigations into murder cases, over the past five or six years, you should not get too conceited in your approach to me and the job. That smartarse attitude cuts no ice. I expect you to carry out the specific order I gave you in connection with the finding of Katrina Chancey, which was that, in the course of your other work, you should try and find out her whereabouts. By inference, I meant that you should find her *alive*. There isn't enough evidence to declare that she's dead. All right?'

It wasn't all right, but Angel thought he had adequately made his point. He didn't say anything.

'You have still the unsolved murder of that wig maker, Peter Wolff, which you seem to be dancing around. You are wasting far too much time chasing shadows. Also, from your report, you seem to have got a tangled interest in a missing man, Grainger . . . spending a lot of time interviewing the wife . . . what's her name? Zoe Grainger? Young, is she? Pretty, is she? Lonely?'

It was Angel's turn to be rattled. His lips tightened back against his teeth. His self-control was now being tested.

'Leave my private life out of this.'

Harker smiled like a snake after a kill.

'I've been there, lad. It's not for you. Stick with what you know about. Take my tip. Don't go wandering into unfamiliar territory.'

Angel stood up. He'd had enough and, anyway, he thought that was the end of the sermon.

Harker stood up and said, 'One more thing. There is every reason to believe that Katrina Chancey is alive and well.

So, I am specifically ordering you not to knock anything else down or do any more digging in Frank Chancey's garden or grounds or . . . anywhere near him.'

Angel came out of Harker's office with the superintendent's last words ringing in his ears.

* * *

He belted down the corridor to his office, furious; he was now more determined than ever to find the missing Katrina Chancey, dead or alive.

There was a knock at the door. It was Gawber.

'You wanted me, sir?'

'Come in. Sit down. Just had a rocket from Harker. Been warned off Chancey. I've been told in no uncertain terms not to question him. The order comes down from the chief. They're drinking mates . . . or something.'

Gawber looked at him.

'Gives me a job, then ties my hands,' Angel growled. 'So many questions. Why would Chancey slyly drop Katrina's phone in the foundations of the fountain when it was being built, then later ring out the number deliberately when I was passing it?'

'How do you know he did either of those things?'

'He or the murderer, who might be one and the same, would be the only person to get near her phone, during or after he had murdered her. Come on, Ron. Is that logical or not?'

'It's logical, sir. But there are other possibilities.'

'For example?'

'Well, sir, say she lost her phone, left it in a taxi, next customer found it and took it . . . used it . . . gave it her boyfriend who happened to work for the concrete mixing company that delivered the ready-mix that was poured there the other day and it dropped out of his pocket into the—'

Angel sighed. 'That's a bit farfetched. And I suppose someone happened to dial her number just as I was walking past the fountain.'

'Well, how do *you* explain that? It must have been coincidence.'

'I've told you about coincidence! No. As I was passing the fountain, the great man was in his study. It overlooks the fountain. He looked down on me, saw me passing the fountain . . . and thought, what a wheeze! I'll take the mick out of that cocky inspector. Pull him down a peg or two. Make him think that Katrina is under the fountain, and I'll laugh my socks off if he decides to demolish it for nothing. That'll put him in a bad way with his superiors and he'll have to watch his step. And I'll be able to bawl him out. And he won't *dare* to look where her body really is.'

Gawber frowned, rubbed his chin and said, 'And where is the body, then?'

'Where do *you* think?'

Gawber rubbed his chin. 'I don't know. Somewhere near the house?'

'Got to be. That Saturday morning, the fourteenth, we weren't able to find a hire car, a taxi or anybody else who had who taken her away from the house to the airport or anywhere else. I don't think she went anywhere. She was dead by then and she's around the house or gardens somewhere now.'

Gawber suddenly piped up. 'She'll be under the gazebo.'

Angel nodded and smiled. 'That was the next place I thought of.'

* * *

The sun was shining and it was quite warm for early May.

The brand-new gazebo was a pretty white wooden circular building with a tiled roof. It stood proudly on top of a great mound of earth, with steps up the side from a lawn recently put down in rolls of turf.

Angel and Gawber made the twenty-eight steps from the lawn. A less strenuous approach was from the house along a path on flagstones through an arbour of roses.

Angel stepped on to the wooden floor of the gazebo. He took in a deep breath and gazed out in each direction in turn. It was in a high position that gave a long view to the south and west of the countryside leading to the Pennines, eastwards a closer view of Tiverton Hall, the lake, the tennis courts and the greenhouses, with farmland beyond, northwards, it was screened from the house by thick evergreen bushes and coniferous trees.

'Do you think Chancey would approve of us trespassing in his garden, standing inside his brand-new gazebo, sir?'

'He'd be delighted. In fact, I bet he's in his office now thinking that that's exactly where he hoped I would be.'

'You mean . . . walking over his wife's grave? Katrina Chancey's body is under here, isn't she?'

Angel peered at him. 'You said she was, Ron.'

'I thought you agreed?'

'No. I didn't say that. I said that that was the next place I'd thought of.'

'Have you changed your mind then, sir?'

'My mind wasn't made up, but I believe that Chancey would think that. After the embarrassment over the fountain, the next place we would think of looking would be the gazebo.'

'Is that what you're going to do then, sir? Take this thing to pieces. It's only timber. And get the bulldozers in?'

'No.'

Their attention was suddenly taken by a small van appearing through the main gate, travelling slowly and uncertainly along the drive towards the house. On the side of the van were the painted words: *Alf Palmer. Plumber, Electrician. The man you can trust.* They thought nothing more of it, but it had disturbed their train of thought.

Angel took a last look round the views. 'Come on, Ron. There's nothing else for us here.'

Gawber stamped on the floorboards several times before turning to join him.

They began the descent and saw another van of a different colour. It was also making an uncertain approach to the house. On the side of the van was painted the words: *Ken Podmore. Plumber. Bathrooms and kitchens fitted.*

By the time they reached the bottom step another van had appeared through the main gate. It was yet another plumber's van with a different name. Angel managed to flag the driver down. A man with three days' growth of beard pulled down the window and said, 'Got here as soon as I could. Couldn't find you, mate. Are you Mr Clancey? It is cash, isn't it?'

Angel said, 'The man's name's Chancey. We're security. My name's Mark Twain. What do you want?'

The man pulled a face. 'Don't tell me it's a hoax? I thought it was funny.'

'What's that?' Angel said.

'Got a message from this man, Clancey or Chancey or whatever. He said he'd give me a thousand quid if I came out straight away. He only wants me to change a U bend. If this is a wind-up, mate, I'll give whoever it is a piece of my mind. I'll tell you, I've got good paying punters waiting for me all over. I thought it was too good to be true. He said it was cash. Honest. I thought it was straight up.'

'That's all right. Carry straight on.'

The man's face brightened. 'Oh great! Yes. Right. Ta, mate.'

The van rattled off towards the house.

Gawber frowned and looked at Angel. He was about to say something when another van came through the gates, passed in front of them and headed tentatively down the drive.

'Must have lost something very valuable down his U bend, sir?'

'That's four plumbers. That's four thousand pounds Chancey's handing out for something.'

'Or maybe it's the first plumber there gets the money?' Gawber said.

Angel wrinkled his nose. 'Very strange, Ron. Very strange.'

* * *

There was a knock at the door. 'Come in,' he called.

It was DS Crisp.

The muscles on Angel's face tightened. 'Where the hell have you been?'

Crisp's jaw dropped. 'Ahmed said you wanted me, sir.'

'I've been wanting you for the last day. You were supposed to be acting security on that safe at Wolff's. What happened to you?'

'I didn't realize you wanted me to stay on there, sir. I've cases and stuff mounting on my desk I needed to do.'

'I know you're busy, lad. We're all busy, but if there's any suggestion that something in that safe is missing, Don Taylor could be in dead trouble. Don't you ever think, lad? And what's the matter with your mobile? Do you sit in a tunnel all day?'

'No sir. It's working all right, I think.'

'It doesn't work all right when I ring you. If it isn't all right, dump it and get another and tell Ahmed the number. All right?'

'All right, sir.'

'Now I have a very special job for you. Could be a matter of life and death. And I want you to stick at. Don't leave it in the middle. No misunderstandings. Got it?'

'Got it, sir.'

Angel quickly gave him his instructions and sent him on his way. He sometimes had doubts about Crisp's commitment to the job. Something he never had to worry about with Ron Gawber or young Ahmed Ahaz. He sighed, ran his hand across his face, leaned forward in the office chair, reached out for the phone and tapped in a number.

'West Yorkshire police.'

'Firearms training officer, please.'

There was a click and a voice said, 'FTO. Sergeant Pepper.'

'DI Angel of Bromersley. I want a hundred thunder-flashes and ten metres of timing fuse wire, minute per metre, please.'

'Sounds as if you're going to have a cracking time, sir. Didn't know you had facilities for a night exercise in Bromersley?'

'Oh yes,' Angel said. 'I am improvising in the huge garden of a local VIP. Have a few new recruits . . . want to break them in . . . let them know what they might expect, downtown here on a Saturday night.'

'How soon do you want the stuff, sir?'

'Today, if possible.'

'Can do. It'll be late this afternoon.'

Angel's tail was wagging. He was delighted. His plan was in motion. There was nothing quite like actually doing something positive and potentially successful, after failure and embarrassment.

He broke the connection and tapped in another number.

'Hello. Is that Ahmed?'

'Yes, sir.'

'I want you to ask Don Taylor to call in to see me. Then Ron Gawber. It's urgent.'

'Right, sir.'

'And then nip downtown, lad, and buy me four lady's shower caps.'

'Shower caps,' Ahmed said slowly. 'Lady's shower caps. Four. Right, sir. What colour?'

'Any colour,' Angel growled.

He broke the connection and then tapped in another number. It was soon answered.

'Leeds Police. SA team. DS Maroney speaking.'

* * *

It was ten minutes to six when Angel arrived home. He walked into the kitchen, went to the fridge, took out a bottle of German beer, picked up a glass off the draining board and walked into the hall. There was no sign of Mary. From the warm, heavy atmosphere in the kitchen he had noticed the oven was on and that two pans were bubbling on the gas ring, making steam, so she wouldn't be far away.

In the hall he saw the monstrous, shabby three legged 'Chippendale' table still supported by the pile of ill-assorted books. He shook his head and wrinkled up his face. He turned away from it and called out, 'Is anybody there?'

Mary came out of the pantry. Without looking at him, she said, 'You're late.'

He stepped back into the kitchen and sniffed.

'Is it ready, then?'

'No.'

'Well, I'm not late then, am I?'

'Tea in this house is five-thirty.'

'Tea in this house is when we want it,' he said bluntly and turned into the sitting room.

He put down the beer and the bottle, took off his jacket, loosened his tie and sat down.

A few minutes later Mary came into the room. 'You might as well know that I've been all over Bromersley and there isn't a single joiner or carpenter, whatever the difference is, that will make me a matching leg for that table.'

Angel thought it sounded as if she wanted peace. The comment was still about that damned table, but she was being reasonable and rational. It was nearing an admission that buying that rickety wooden pile had not been a good idea. He must think quickly about what to reply. It had been a bumpy weekend. He would welcome a truce. He poured the beer slowly.

'What do you propose to do then?' he said eventually.

'Well, I haven't given up hope yet. I wondered if you knew anywhere?'

He knew she was thorough. If she couldn't find anywhere, there wasn't anywhere. He sipped the beer.

'No, love. I don't know anybody. And what do they say?'

'Most have said they haven't time. But I think that they can't be bothered. Too small a job for them.'

'Of course, there is a bit of skill required. I noticed the leg tapers most of the way down until near the bottom when it swells out. It would take quite a bit of time and skill to copy it. And it would be a one off. Did you try Smith's?'

'First place I went to.'

There must be somebody who could and would be willing to make a fourth leg for that table. He screwed up his face. 'Try wider afield. Try Sheffield.'

'That's what I thought,' she said, her face brightening. 'First thing tomorrow. There must be *somebody*.'

He looked down into the beer. His suggestion to try Sheffield was not such a brilliant idea. She'd be having him troop over there, messing about with unknown tradesmen of doubtful parentage who would be into the business of charging fantasy prices. There was still £106 of that legacy not yet spent. It would be good if he could avoid that being frittered away. It would do very nicely against the gas bill.

'Would you like to lay the table?' she called from the kitchen. 'It will only be a couple of minutes.'

'Right, love.'

They had the meal, watched some unfunny repeats of unfunny comedy shows followed by the news featuring death, disaster, famine and cruelty on television until half past ten. Then Angel yawned.

'At midnight I have to go out on a job with Ron Gawber.'

Mary's face dropped. She wasn't pleased. 'Working nights now?'

'No. Just having a bit of trouble getting some evidence. I expect to get positive proof tonight.'

'How long will you be?'

'Around a couple of hours, I expect.'

'Not dangerous, is it?' she said. 'I don't know why I ask. You always say no.'

He smiled. 'No.'

She smiled.

Peace seemed at last to be restored in the Angel household.

FOURTEEN

The church clock chimed a quarter past midnight.

The streets of Bromersley were still, dry and quiet. The pubs were shut, the drunks and the good were in bed. Only policemen, nurses, doctors, shift workers, ambulance drivers, murderers and thieves were roaming the streets.

Angel stopped the BMW outside 12 Royston Avenue, Bromersley. The door of the house promptly opened and out slipped Ron Gawber. He crossed the deserted flagstone pavement and got into the car.

The two men were on a mission. And it wasn't legal. There was a certain sort of excitement in the air. The two men sensed it in each other.

Angel's forehead was moist and he could hear his pulse beat in his ears, while Gawber was grinning nervously, like a newly appointed cabinet minister out on the pull.

'You don't have to do this, you know, Ron. If anything goes wrong, we could both finish up out on our ear.'

'Long time since I went out at night, sir. This has got to be better than telly. Also, be good to get that chap behind bars. Too smart. Too complacent by far. You've got more to lose. I'm only going to be trespassing and causing a nuisance. You are the one committing the actual breaking and entering.'

'Only entering, Ron. I hope not to be breaking in as well.'

He drove under the yellow halogen lights past rows of small, quiet, dark, respectable houses, up to the Rotherham Road traffic lights, turned left and along to Jubilee Park, which was off Creesforth Road. He drove on to the big free car park there and parked up. He was pleased to see two other cars parked there in the night; his car wouldn't be so conspicuous.

He turned to Gawber, licked his lips and said, 'Let's go through it again, Ron. Make absolutely sure we know what we're about.'

'Right, sir. Well, we have a hundred thunderflashes. We string them together to ignite in quick succession in sticks of twenty, then position two sticks near the fountain base, right under his bedroom window on the car park, twenty more in the bushes, twenty more in the gazebo and twenty near the main gate.'

'That's it.'

Gawber nodded. 'Right. And I move from point to point and ignite them on a short fuse of a minute or so.'

'Aye. The zigzag sequence of the locations means that you will not only be ahead of them and catch them by surprise, but you will also always be able to move to the next location in the dark and so not be seen.'

'I'm glad of that, sir.'

'You must *not* be seen. He may very well have a gun.'

Gawber's eyebrows shot up.

'After you have ignited the last stick at the main gate,' Angel continued, 'you return here to the car and wait for me.'

'Right, sir.'

'And in each case, don't hang about waiting for the thunderflashes to ignite. Light the timing fuse and get to the next position in the dark. After the last position at the gate, light the fuse and run like hell.'

Gawber grinned. 'Like Hendon, sir?'

'Damned sight more serious,' Angel replied. 'And dangerous,' he added. 'Got your stopwatch, torch, shower caps, gloves and box of matches?'

'Yes, sir.'

'When you get back here, switch on your mobile in case I want to phone you. And I'll give you my car remote so that you can get in the car. All right? Come on. Let's go.'

'Hang on a minute, sir. What shall I do if you don't get back?'

Angel smiled. 'I'll be back, Ron,' he said confidently. 'I shouldn't be more than ten minutes behind you. And let's hope that this time, we nail the bastard.'

* * *

It was 2.17 a.m. Zero hour.

Angel scampered across the edge of the gravel car park and hid around the corner of the house. This was a very delicate manoeuvre. He knew if he was caught, he could be arrested, charged and thrown out of the force. It didn't bear thinking about. He stood with his back pressed against the wall. His chest quivered like ten thousand bees doing whatever bees do.

Gawber ignited the fuse of the first stick of thunderflashes.

Seconds later, the peace and quiet of the car park under Frank Chancey's bedroom window became as noisy and as bright as the launch of a rocket to Mars.

His bedroom light went on. A few seconds after that Frank Chancey's face appeared at the window. By then the thunder-flashes had burned out. In the darkness, he could see nothing. Three minutes after that, Lyle's head peered out. He must have heard the racket and gone to his boss's room.

Both puzzled faces withdrew.

Angel, in the darkness took two shower caps out of a pocket and put one over each foot, then tore open an envelope and pulled on a pair of rubber gloves.

From the concealment of the bushes Gawber, also wearing shower caps and rubber gloves, crept up to at the edge of the car park and ignited the two-minute fuse to the second stick of thunderflashes then moved swiftly to the clump of bushes at the other side of the drive further away from the house.

Chancey and Lyle returned to the bedroom window and caught the full sight and blast of twenty thunderflashes firing in quick succession on the car park below. Three or four minutes after that the main door of the house banged open and both men appeared in night attire. Chancey was waving a shotgun, and Lyle was brandishing a powerful flashlight. They searched the car park area then began searching the nearby bushes.

While they were busy searching Angel came round from the shadow of the corner of the house, sprinted across the front of it, through the open door, into the hall and up the stairs. He rushed along the landing to Chancey's bedroom. Then, much to his surprise, outside the bedroom door, he saw exactly what he had come for: Chancey's shoes. They would be the ones that he would have worn that day, no doubt placed there for the versatile Lyle to clean. Without delay, Angel snatched them up, rushed into the bathroom, found the light switch, pulled it and crossed to the washbasin. He heard the last stick of thunderflashes explode and reckoned he must be a little behind schedule. He took a small glass bottle of the powerful acid and two small pieces of plastic sponge out of his pocket and put them on the edge of the sink. He rubbed one of the sponges on the soap in the soap dish and roughly washed the shoe soles, then rinsed them under the tap. He then poured the concentrated acid on to the other small piece of sponge, wiped each shoe sole and held the shoes together up to the light, looking for a reaction. He expected a bubbling or a colour to show. He waited. There was nothing! Nothing on either shoe sole. His jaw muscles tightened. His stomach turned over. The bees returned. He quickly made the test again. And stared at the shoes. Still no reaction. This was a disaster. There was nothing more to do. He licked his lips. He heard the last stick of thunderflashes go up. He must pack up and get out of there. He rinsed the shoe soles under the cold tap, grabbed a nearby towel and wiped them dry. Then he dropped the sponges in the loo and flushed them away, stuffed the bottle back in his pocket, straightened the towel, picked up the shoes and made for the door. He turned, had a quick look round to check that he had left everything in order, pulled the light switch, ran along the landing to Chancey's bedroom, where he deposited the shoes by the door, just as had found them. Then he flew down the stairs, along the hallway to the main entrance, along the front of the house and round the corner. He stood there, his back to the wall, breathing heavily, just in time to hear the sound of two men stomping over the gravel car park.

'We ought to phone the police, sir,' he heard Lyle say.

'No. Only kids having a lark. I reckon we've chased them off. They won't come back.'

'Oh no, sir. Those firecrackers must cost a few bob. And there was a lot of 'em. It was too well organized, first here and then there. Had us racing around like March hares.'

'What could the police do?'

'Well, what did the skylarkers want?'

'I don't know, Jimmy.'

'Can I get you a drink, sir. Get you back to sleep?'

The door slammed. Silence.

Angel waited a few minutes to make certain that Chancey and Lyle had settled down for the rest of the night. Then he made his way uneventfully back to his car; it took him about ten minutes. He opened the door, slumped into the seat, closed the door and turned to a smiling Gawber.

'Did you get it, sir?'

Angel sighed. 'No. Negative. I must have got hold of the wrong shoes.'

Gawber's head came up. 'Either that or you got the right shoes, sir, and Chancey didn't murder Peter Wolff.'

'It's more than a week since Wolff died; he's had plenty of time to dispose of them. He's not a fool. If he didn't murder Peter Wolff, I haven't the faintest idea who did. I'm fed up with this case, Ron. There are no clues, no evidence, no witnesses and no motive.'

'It'll have to go in that big, fat file of unsolved murders, sir.'

Angel's jaw muscles tightened. 'Not while it's on my list, it won't.'

Gawber smiled. He knew Angel refused to be beaten. He had a hundred per cent success rate at solving murders. The hierarchy at Bromersley were quietly quite proud of his record and all murder cases or suspected murder cases were always directed to him.

'I will now have to find another line of inquiry,' he grunted.

'And another suspect,' Gawber said.

Angel yawned. 'My bed's calling me,' he said and he reached out to the ignition switch.

* * *

It was expected that if you were on DI Angel's team, and had spent half a night on duty, that you would still check in by 8.28 a.m. the following morning as usual. There was a slight buffering consolation: those ranks below inspector were paid overtime. Those who were inspector or higher simply received the glory. However there wasn't a lot of it about in Bromersley nick that morning. The only reward on offer to Angel was a decent cup of tea.

'Ta, lad,' he said, as Ahmed placed the saucer on the improvised table mat. It was a CD with the words 'How to get broadband with BT' printed on the reverse side.

Angel picked up the phone and tapped in a number. As the phone rang out he turned to Ahmed and said, 'Nip up to the SOCO office and ask Don Taylor if he's got Katrina Chancey's SIM card sorted. It's time I was hearing from him.'

'Right, sir,' Ahmed said. He went out and closed the door.

There was a click in the telephone earpiece and a deep warm woman's voice said, 'Hello, Zoe Grainger. Who is that?'

'Inspector Angel here, Zoe. Good morning. I'm sorry I haven't any news of your husband just yet. Just wanted to ask you a couple of questions.'

She sighed. 'Oh, really, Inspector. He has never been away so long. I really do suspect the worst. I honestly think he's dead. There's no other explanation. Whatever am I going to do?'

'I am really sorry, Zoe.'

'I can't believe he would stay with another woman as long as this. Once he's made love to her, and dominated her, he immediately loses interest. I've seen it a thousand times. Oh, Inspector what am I going to do? I can't go on like this. Waiting. Just waiting. I've no money, and the gas bill's arrived this morning. I can't go on like this. I'll have to go back to work.'

He knew all about bills, especially gas bills. It was the old Micawber principle. Money was no problem to those who had enough, but it was an absolute disaster to those who hadn't. He scratched his head. How on earth was he going to direct her attention to his questions? 'Go down to Social Security. Tell them your trouble. I am sure they will help.'

'I am always down there. They don't believe me anymore. But I will have to go there. They'll only tell me I should be working. It's such an embarrassment. I tell you, Inspector, this time, when he comes back . . . if he comes back, I swear, I'll kill him.'

Angel thought, a confession before a crime . . . that's unusual. He couldn't find the right words. 'I'm very sorry, Zoe.'

'I shouldn't be bothering you with this, Inspector. I'm sorry. You . . . you phoned up just as I was about to explode. I feel better. I've got it out of my system. Now what is it? You wanted to ask me something?'

'Yes. It was about his credit cards and . . .'

'Huh! You must be joking. He doesn't have credit cards. He used to have a whole lot of them in folding plastic cellophane fronted wallets, which he used to enjoy unfastening and watching them unroll down to the floor. He had enough cards for Dodworth Colliery Band to play a full game of gin rummy. Huh! They won't let him have credit cards again,

Inspector. Nobody gives Gabriel credit if they ever want to see their money again.'

'I suppose he doesn't have a bank account?'

'His name is mud at every bank in Bromersley.'

'He doesn't have any savings in a post office, building society or anywhere?'

'Hell, no.'

'Mobile phone?'

'When the initial money ran out, he didn't have any cash to put any more time on the thing, so he chucked it in the canal.'

'So there's nothing we can look at that might tell us where he is or what he might have done since the night he got on that train at Bromersley station nearly four weeks ago?'

'I've told you, Inspector, he's dead!'

He suddenly heard her crying. She let out a big wail.

He sighed and bit his lip. He struggled to think of something comforting to say. His chest swelled, became unpleasantly hot and prickly.

'Don't go on like that, Zoe,' he said eventually.

'The most beautiful man . . . in the world and he's dead . . . because I just couldn't hold on to him.' There was more sniffling.

'There, there,' Angel said.

There was a moment's silence then she suddenly said firmly, 'I've finished, Inspector. Not another tear. That's it. I'm sorry to have embarrassed you. You are very kind. Don't worry about me. I am going to get a job. I am going straight out to the employment office, and I'll get a *Chronicle*. I'll get something. I enjoyed it when I was working, before. I don't see why I shouldn't enjoy it again. I may be a bit rusty and I know they . . . nobody would give me a sub. But . . . but . . . that bloody gas bill will have to wait a week or two. That's all.'

He felt exactly the same about his gas bill.

'Was there anything else you wanted me for, Inspector?'

'No. Take it steady now, Zoe. There's no solid reason to believe that Gabriel is dead. Any day, any time now, he could come walking back into your life as large as—'

'If he does, I'll kill him,' she bawled angrily. 'I *will*, I'll *kill* him. Putting me through all this.'

Angel smiled. 'All right, Zoe?' he said gently. 'All right?'

She simmered down. 'All right, Inspector,' she sighed. 'All right. And thank you.'

He replaced the phone slowly, still holding on to it. He shook his head thoughtfully as he considered where Gabriel Grainger might really be. He had told Zoe that he had thought her husband was all right, but he didn't really know. He had nothing to go on. He simply hoped that he was somewhere safe. It sounded as if the death of that pretty useless husband of hers would hardly be possible for her to bear. He had seen this situation many times before. And telling someone that their loved one was dead was one of the saddest parts of the job. He only hoped to goodness that there had not been another murder, that Gabriel Grainger was safe, and that it was not long before he had the murderer of Peter Wolff safely under lock and key.

He was still brooding over this when there was a knock at the door. He looked up. 'Come in.'

It was Taylor. He bustled in waving a scrappy piece of A4. 'The results on Katrina Chancey's mobile phone that you were chasing, sir.'

'Ah yes. Sit down, Don.'

'Yes, sir. They're only handwritten. I'll tidy it up and let you have a typed-up copy later.'

'Any prints on the outside case, Don?'

'The case had been wiped clean, sir, and of course we rinsed the sludge off carefully, slowly with a fine spray of chilled water so as to save any prints, but there simply weren't any.'

Angel nodded. 'Yes. And what did you find out?'

'She was a very busy on the phone. Mostly calls to her agency in London, Top Notch.'

'Yes I know of it. Any messages?'

'No, sir. There were calls to a dressmaker in Leeds. One to her husband.'

'Any to Grainger's number. I'm interested to know if there was any contact between Gabriel Grainger and Katrina Chancey.'

'No, sir. Not on this phone. And no calls were made from it after Friday, April the thirteenth. The latest calls were made to it from her agency, from her husband and lastly from you, sir.'

'Mmm. The last two were made when the phone was buried under the fountain. The call ring that I heard was the result of Chancey dialling her number from his study as he was observing me through his window admiring the fountain. It could only have been he who dropped her phone, with malice aforethought, under the foundations of the fountain.'

FIFTEEN

Superintendent Harker looked up. 'I've a lot on. What do you want?' he bawled as he shuffled some of the papers on his littered desk.

Angel stared across the office at him as he closed the door. He thought what a horrible spectacle Harker looked in his off the peg Netto suit, two sizes too big, the Victorian waterspout nose, the white bald head and the big ginger eyebrows. He could see him in Jim Henson's Muppets orchestra playing the double bass.

'Just heard from SOCO, sir. Their findings from Katrina Chancey's SIM card from her mobile show that Frank Chancey dialled his wife's mobile phone deliberately so that I would hear it as I passed the fountain.'

'So what?'

'So . . . that's why . . . obviously I had to dig up the fountain, expecting to find Katrina's body.'

'But her body wasn't there. You made a bloody fool of me! And the chief constable, and the force. It was an embarrassment all round. It was in the papers, you know. "*Police ruin*

170

eighty-thousand-pound Fountain". *"Singeing In The Rain."* I've read all the tabloid headlines. They don't do the force any good.'

'No, sir. It was Chancey. Chancey who made a fool of all of us. And I've worked out his reason for doing it. He reckoned that we would be so embarrassed at not finding his wife's body there that we wouldn't dig anywhere else for fear of any more embarrassment.'

Harker lowered the big eyebrows. 'A man can phone his wife whenever he wants to, can't he? He doesn't need the permission of a particular detective inspector of police, does he? If it unfortunately rings as you happen to be passing by, it hardly makes him into a murderer.'

'Under these circumstances, sir, it might. Because once he had made a fool of us by inciting us to dig up the fountain, he could safely hide his wife's body almost anywhere close by, confident that we dare not risk being embarrassed by a second futile excavation. Don't you see?'

'No, lad. I don't see. You didn't *have* to dig up the fountain in the first place.'

'Well, it—'

'Look here, lad. You were only briefed to cast an eye over the disappearance of this woman. It is not a murder case. It will never be a murder case. Frank Chancey is a highly respectable businessman, gives to charity, pays his taxes, doesn't chase women, keeps his nose clean. His flighty, pretty, nay beautiful, wife runs off, with or without a younger man. That's all there is to it. He is not master criminal Peter Sutcliffe. You are crediting Frank Chancey with a mind as devious and crackpot as yours is. You're always coming in my office with these ridiculous nutcase ideas. I don't know where you get them from. You went to local schools, didn't you? Had local teaching, didn't you? You weren't over-educated. Didn't suffer the

171

disadvantages of a modern university education, get stuffed up with modern idealistic tripe, and outlandish political ideas invoked by long-haired weirdos. There's no insanity in your family that we don't know about, is there? I know you've had the odd success with a difficult case in the past, but this is getting ridiculous.'

'All I wanted to ask, was—'

'I suppose you want permission to knock Chancey's house down. I suppose that's what all this preamble is leading to. Or sink a mine shaft in his garden.'

* * *

Angel tramped up the pea green painted corridor back to his office, his mind in a whirl. Trying to discuss a case with the super was nearly as difficult as convincing Mary that paying the gas bill was more important that buying an ugly battered table with three legs for the hall because there's a slight chance that it might be a Chippendale masterpiece.

The phone rang. It was the woman civilian on the switchboard who curtly told him that DS Maroney of Leeds SA team wanted to speak to him. He blinked, looked up and asked her to put him through straight away.

'Yes, Sergeant, have you found something?' he said urgently.

'It's not a body, sir. It's a heavy metal thing, like a metal suit. It showed up on the scanner.'

He grasped what he meant. 'Is it a suit of armour?'

'Yes, sir. That's it. A suit of armour. Right in the middle of the lake, at about the deepest point, well covered in mud.'

Angel smiled. It wasn't what they were looking for, but it was a welcome find. Lord Tiverton would be pleased. 'Can you get it up?'

'Oh yes, sir. I just wondered if it mattered, whether we should leave it or not?'

Angel smiled. 'Oh no, bring it up, please. And don't damage it. It's supposed to be worth millions.'

Maroney grunted. 'Millions? Really?'

Angel replaced the phone and rubbed his chin. He hadn't expected to see the missing suit of armour again. He expected it would have been sold abroad somewhere and would be in somebody's private collection, possibly in some exotic millionaire's penthouse. It seemed ridiculous for thieves to steal it from Lord Tiverton's outbuilding like that simply to dump it 200 yards away in the middle of his lake. What was the sense in that? And to steal a wheelbarrow, presumably in which to wheel it. He scratched his head. He recalled that the robbery took place while the Tivertons were away. They were in Scotland that Saturday, 14 April, when Katrina Chancey went missing.

Suddenly Angel's mouth dropped open as the ball rolled along into the hole, the light went green and the bell rang. He dashed out of his office, down the corridor, past the cells and out of the back door of the station to the car park.

He was at Tiverton Hall in a matter of minutes. He saw the Range Rover with the words Leeds Police Sub Aqua Team on the door by the outbuildings and parked the BMW alongside. He made his way down the crazy paving to the little quay, past the sub aqua team's trailer, to where the motorboat was moored. He could see DS Maroney and another frogman in the water winching the suit of armour into an inflatable in the middle of the lake. He called out to them and waved. They were too busy to respond. A few minutes later he heard their outboard start up and splutter its way towards the little jetty. It arrived with its gruesome burden.

Their faces told the story.

'There's a dead body inside this suit of armour, sir.'

Angel nodded. He had known it.

* * *

The phone rang. He picked it up. It was Crisp. There was something very wrong. He sounded anxious.

'What's the matter, lad?' Angel said, his hand shaking.

'I've lost him, sir. I am at Scotch Corner on the A1. I don't know whether he went straight on or turned off on the A66. He's in a red Ferrari, sir. He's been doing a hundred and forty. I tried to keep up with him. I don't know how far you want me to go. And I shall need some petrol soon.'

Angel's lips tightened back against his teeth.

He was a very worried man.

'All right, lad. Come back here, pronto.'

He replaced the phone, reached into his inside pocket for an old envelope, found a number on it, replaced it, picked up the phone and tapped the number in.

The deep, breathy voice of Zoe Grainger said, 'Yes? Who is that?'

'Inspector Angel here,' he said trying to sound bright and breezy. 'Just wondered how you were getting along.'

She stiffened. 'You don't have to be gentle with me, Inspector. Something's happened. Have you some news about Gabriel?'

'No. No. Nothing.'

'You can tell me. I can take it.'

'There's nothing. I just think that for your comfort and peace of mind, you should move to our . . . police house for a couple of days, that's all.'

Her voice hardened. 'What's the matter? What's happening? You think *I'm* in danger now. What is it? You *must* tell me.'

He licked his lips. 'Just a precaution. Yes, it is possible that Gabriel might be having . . . a difficult time. If you come to our safe house, we can at least make sure that—'

'I want to know what's happening, Inspector. No more of this prevarication. What the bloody hell's going on?'

He would have to tell her. There was no wrapping it up. 'Your husband may be in danger, Zoe. As we have no idea where he is we can't protect him. Now, he may be perfectly safe. In any event, I am sure he will return home quite soon—'

'I'll stay here. I need to be here. If he's on his way home, I need to be here . . . to welcome him.'

'That's not possible. He may be followed. I intend to have a welcoming committee waiting for the man following him.'

'What would anybody want him for? Settle an old score? He can handle himself, Inspector. He does regular workouts. Who is this man?'

'It's serious, Zoe. Very serious. It may only be for a day or so.'

'When did you say you expect him back?'

'I can't be sure. But soon, I think. Very soon.'

'Oh God!'

He managed to calm her down and terminate the call. He immediately summoned WPC Baverstock. He instructed her to go to Flat 4, Jubilee Close, help Zoe Grainger pack some things for one night, leave the flat door unlocked and transfer her to the safe house on Beechfield Walk, and to stay with her a while and settle her in.

She rushed off.

He then summoned DC Scrivens.

'You wanted me, sir?'

'Yes, lad. Do you know Gabriel Grainger?'

Scrivens frowned, then looked up. 'Tall, bronzed, athletic, black hair, sir? Defrauding a woman out of money? Is that him? I was one of the arresting officers who brought him in, a couple of years back.'

'It was five years back. Yes, that's him. Time is short. I want you and John Weightman to draw handguns and six rounds each, and go quickly round to his home at Flat 4, Jubilee Close. Go in an unmarked car and keep out of sight. There should be nobody in and the door unlocked. Go inside, leave it unlocked and find places to hide. If Grainger turns up, for his safety I want you to bring him straight here. Also, he may be followed by a man, who may be armed; if he turns up, arrest him and bring him in. I warn you, you must defend yourselves and Grainger against him at all times. He could be extremely dangerous. All right?'

'Yes, sir.'

Scrivens went out. The door closed.

Angel could feel his blood pumping round. A tight pain in his chest came to him at times like this. He stood up, took a few deep breaths then reached out for the phone.

'Ahmed. I'm going down to Lord Tiverton's place, Tiverton Hall, if anybody wants me. I'll be on my mobile.'

'Right, sir.'

He arrived to find the whole police circus in full sway: the white marquee set up on the side of the lake near the jetty, the Range Rovers with their flashing lights, the blue-and-white tape, the big white SOCO van, Dr Mac's discreet silver-grey car, the Leeds police sub aqua team's vehicle and trailer, the police dog handler's van and the hospital's black body-wagon.

Angel parked his BMW further away from the concentration of activity, in front of the outbuildings, and walked swiftly down to the marquee. A dog barked excitedly. A PC threw up a salute, he responded, dodged under the DO NOT CROSS tape, pulled open the flap on the marquee and went in. The smell was appalling. There were three men in whites, boots and masks. He recognized the shortest man. It was Dr Mac. Nobody spoke. Mac was closing his bag. Next to him, on a stretcher-bed on wheels, was a naked chalk-white assemblage of most of a once human body comprising long legs, skinny arms hanging from a torso, where a head had been was an horrific blue and red mishmash half-covered in straggly wet hair.

Angel's jaw dropped. He turned away.

One of the men pulled a sheet over the corpse.

Mac caught Angel's eye and pointed to the flap, indicating that he was going out.

Angel preceded him and held open the flap. Outside the air smelled of gardenias. They walked up the rise, under the tape and along the path to the outbuildings.

Mac pulled his mask down under his chin and said, 'Nasty. I fear I might never find the actual blow that killed her. There are so many. Face and mouth area severely damaged, finger-ends and thumbs removed . . .'

Angel sighed. 'Presumably to conceal the identity.'

'Aye. Long time since I saw anything as extreme as this.'

'Female.'

'Age, at a guess, between sixteen and thirty-five. I'll get more exact after examination. Blonde, of course. Blue eyes. Tall. About five feet eight or nine. No obvious signs of drugs. No obvious signs that she put up a struggle, either. One severe blow to the temple or crown and out she would be.' He shook his head. 'A great pity.'

Angel nodded. They had both seen this many times before. Angel knew he'd never get used to it.

'We're taking the victim to the mortuary now, Michael, unless there's anything more you want to see?'

'How was the body put into the suit of armour?'

'Easily enough. Back opens up on a hinge. Murderer would simply thread the arms into the sleeves, push the torso in and close the back . . . like a cupboard. The legs, each into a steel leg. They weren't fastened to the top bit. The head simply put on from the top. The gauntlets and bits that cover the feet weren't used, or they fell off. The divers pulled them out, and a wheelbarrow. Being steel it showed on the scan.'

Angel nodded. 'Mmm. Did they pull anything else out? The weapon?'

'No.'

'Any ideas?'

'Most probably a ball-pane hammer.'

Taylor came rushing over to him.

'Sir. Sir. We've found some bloodstains on the jetty by the boat.'

A handsome springer spaniel stood on the jetty, his eyes bright and tail going like a helicopter propeller. A proud handler stood by.

Angel went up to him, looked down at the Tarmacadam. There was nothing to see. 'Blood did you say, lad? How do you know?'

'It's Kim, sir. Blood trained. He's never wrong.'

Kim barked. Angel stroked his ears and back.

'It'll be the rain as flushed it away, sir. There's been quite a lot.'

Angel straightened up and rubbed his chin. 'Ta, lad.' He looked at the motor launch and called out to Taylor. 'Have you swabbed the boat, Don?'

Taylor came up to him. 'No, sir.'

'Give it a careful seeing to,' Angel said leaning over it. He admired the gleaming brown varnished wood and white painted aluminium bodywork. 'He must have used it for transporting the body and the suit of armour to the middle of the lake.'

'Right, sir.'

He turned away. 'I must have a word with Lord Tiverton,' he muttered to himself. His mobile phone rang out. He dived into his pocket and pulled it out. It was DC Scrivens.

Angel took a deep breath. He couldn't imagine what was coming next. 'Yes, lad. What's the matter?'

'Grainger's arrived here, sir. He's wounded and he wants to know where his wife is. He's acting up. He refuses to go with us. Do I cuff him or what.'

'What do you mean, he's wounded? How bad is it?'

'Don't know, sir. It's a gunshot wound in his arm. I reckon he should be seen by a doctor, make sure it doesn't go wrong.'

'Right. Take him to the A and E at the General, then. Cuff him if needs be, but make sure he knows that he's not under arrest. Tell him that we are protecting him. And tell him that his wife is in our custody for her safety. All right? And when he's had his arm seen to, give me a ring, and let me know what's happening. All right?'

* * *

'What made you think that Katrina Chancey was buried in the bottom of Lord Tiverton's lake, sir?'

'Well, I wasn't going to be conned into burrowing under Chancey's gazebo and have egg on my face twice. I knew he couldn't have moved the body far, so when his lordship told me his wheelbarrow had also been stolen, an idea emerged. I kept it quiet because I didn't want Chancey to get to know and start making plans to make an early escape attempt. We haven't enough to book him with yet.'

'But why was Grainger shot, sir?' Gawber said. 'I don't understand why Chancey wanted Grainger dead.'

'Don't you see, Ron? At the moment, we can't prove that that body just dragged out of Lord Tiverton's lake is that of Katrina Chancey, but I'd be happy to bet my gas bill with any respectable turf accountant that it most definitely is. However, as we can't *prove* that it's Katrina then she, theoretically, is still alive, and if Gabriel Grainger was actually murdered and his body had been buried in another lake or somewhere else, and nobody knew anything about it, then it could be thought that Gabriel and Katrina had run off together for mad, interminable sex. In which case we, the police, would have no need — indeed, no business — to be out there looking for either of them. They haven't committed a crime, they're over eighteen and are free to "disappear" with the other three thousand people in this country, who vanish every year and are never seen again. That's why Chancey wanted him dead and lost. Got it?'

'Yes, sir.'

'It's called freedom, or liberty or democracy or something like that.'

Gawber nodded. 'Right, sir. It's sad though.'

'*Very* sad . . . that their lives are so miserable living with their wives, partners, mothers, fathers, children or even on their own, they decide that it's a better option. Anyway, what we've got to do now is prove that that messed-up pile of human meat was originally the body of Katrina Chancey.'

The phone rang. It was Scrivens.

'We're at the general hospital, sir. The doctor says Grainger's arm is nasty, but it's only a flesh wound, hasn't touched the bone. As it's a gunshot wound, he has to report it to the superintendent. I suppose that's all right. What do you want us to do with him now, sir?'

'Is he quieter now?'

'Yes sir. The doctor gave him an injection. Told him to rest. He says he feels sleepy.'

Angel frowned. He had intended interviewing Grainger, but it would hardly be fair to him.

'All right. Take him up to the safe house on Beechfield Walk. That's where his wife is. Check him in to WPC Baverstock and leave him there. Tell him that for his own safety he's not to go out, then clock off.'

'Right, sir.'

Angel replaced the phone. He glanced up at the clock. 'It's six o'clock, Ron. Don't know about you. I've had enough of today. I'm going home.'

SIXTEEN

'What you doing late, love?' she said gently as he came through the back door. 'Been trying to stop it drying up for the last hour.'

Angel blinked. Mary was friendly, considering he was late. That was the nicest she had spoken to him since the saga of the 'Chippendale' table had started.

He took off his jacket.

'Yes. Sorry. Found a body . . . a murdered body . . . came in late,' he said as he crossed over to the fridge and took out a bottle of German beer.

She wrinkled her nose and feigned a shudder. 'I don't know why you can't get a respectable job. Instead of all that mixing with sleazy individuals and messing about with dead bodies and their DUD.'

'DNA!'

'DNA? I thought that was a machine that plays recordings of films and things.'

'That's a DVD.'

'No, you're wrong. I know for a fact they're called CDs. My sister's got one in her Jimmy Osmond collection.'

His eyebrows shot up. 'Who?'

She didn't reply. She rattled some plates.

He shook his head. Got a glass from the cupboard and poured the beer while still standing.

'Well, sit down. I'm serving up.'

Despite all the argy-bargy, Angel identified a distinct thawing in the relationship. In fact, she was so agreeable throughout the meal that he began to be quite worried. He thought there must have been some further expensive development concerning the three-legged eyesore in the hall.

It was after they had finished the meal, cleared away, she had kicked off her slippers and before he had sat down in the sitting room and switched on the television, that she began.

'You know that I have tried all over Sheffield to get a matching leg for that table?'

'Yes,' he said, hiding his eyes in the glass of beer, bracing himself for what was coming.

'Well, there's a man on Abbeydale Road. He's an antique dealer. He says he can do it. It'll cost four hundred pounds.'

Angel's heart started pounding. He said nothing. Her stories had a way of building up to a climax, then, it was to be hoped, coming back down to reality. The only money available was £106. It was no use her proposing ideas involving a higher figure. There was no question of extending the mortgage. That was definitely out. He sat tight.

'Yes, love,' he said mildly, hoping the outcome was less than £106.

'Well, Michael, I've spent a lot of time trying to get a matching leg for this table leg,' she said. 'I've phoned all the likely people in Bromersley, Barnsley and Sheffield now, to no avail.'

And it's cost me an absolute fortune in telephone calls too, *he wanted to say but didn't.*

183

'And, in view of the fact that you are against this proposal—'

'I am not against it, we simply can't afford it.'

'In view of the fact that you are against this proposal, I have decided to put it into Williamson's auction, tomorrow evening. That Mr Williamson is such a nice man. He said he'd accept it as a late entry.'

Angel felt his back muscles relax. Mary was referring to a half-baked, gimcrack establishment run by a publican up a backstreet on the outskirts of town. Sending the table to auction would at least get shot of it. Get it out of the house. But she'd get nothing for it in that flea-bitten establishment. She'd be lucky to get a bid of a fiver. That would be £500 down the pan. Timms must be laughing his chrysanthemum-perfumed socks off.

'With the proceeds,' she continued, 'I'll have to satisfy myself with a table from that very modern shop . . . IDEA.'

'You mean, IKEA.'

'Or the FBI.'

He frowned. 'MFI.'

'Yes. Well, anyway, they both sell brand-new modern stuff. Wouldn't be ideal, but there you are.'

He rubbed his chin. What was there to say? It was a *fait accompli*. It was goodbye to £500. But it had been goodbye two weeks ago, when she had first met the sainted Seymour Timms. Anyway, goodbye and good riddance. He hoped that she would learn from the experience. The gas bill would have to wait until his next pay day. Thank goodness it was summer. He wouldn't like to be paying late for gas in the winter. Although he didn't suppose they would cut them off. He wasn't pleased. He didn't like Mary being done like that. He wrinkled his nose, then nodded and picked up the *Radio Times*.

'The thing is . . .' she said and waited.

He eventually looked up at her.

'Would you be a darling and take it round there some-time this evening before eight o'clock?'

His jaw dropped. He sighed, then he stood up. He threw the *Radio Times* on to the chair and said, 'I'll do it now.'

Mary smiled.

It was a treat to see her smile. She hadn't smiled since that cheque had come from Snap, Crackle and Pop.

She stood on the front step and watched him load the tawdry woodworm-ridden three-legged shambles of a table in the boot of the BMW.

'Take the books,' she called, 'and set it up firmly for him. Make the best of it, for me. There's a darling.'

Things were looking up.

He wrapped the tabletop carefully with the cloth, then wrapped it over a leg and pressed everything down. He closed the boot lid.

'Don't let it wobble,' she added. 'Show him how firm it stands and tell him that that nice Mr Seymour Timms from the BBC used to stand his prize chrysanthemums on it. And remind him that it's a Chippendale piece, around 1780. Could have been in the Nostell Priory collection. No. Perhaps you'd better not say that, as I can't be sure about it.'

He sighed. The muscles round his mouth tightened. He loved her dearly, but she really was pushing her luck. He got in the car, started the engine and drove away.

* * *

It was 8.28 a.m.

Angel put his head round the CID office looking for Ahmed. The young man came in behind him.

Angel looked at his watch.

'I'm not late, sir,' Ahmed said, looking wide-eyed.

'No lad, you're not. But there's a lot going to happen today, and I want to be in front of it. I want you to get the Top Notch model agency, London, on the phone for me. I want to speak to a woman called Melanie.'

'Right, sir.'

'And I want you to find DS Gawber, DS Crisp and DC Scrivens and send them to my office, pronto.'

'Right, sir.'

Angel went into his office. He took off his raincoat and hung it on the hook on the stationery cupboard, just as he had done for the past eight years. As he did it, he began thinking. He liked being a copper and he liked being a DI. Detective inspector was the best rank to be. To be any lower meant you might be on relatively menial jobs, even fetching pet cats down trees, while any higher and you would be forever in meetings, grappling with targets, statistics, reports and kow-towing to visiting hierarchy. No. DI was where he was and DI was where he wanted to stay. He would always be hands on, doing what he liked doing best, catching the worst of all criminals: murderers.

The phone rang. He reached out for it. It was the Top Notch model agency.

'Ah, Melanie. We are still looking for Katrina Chancey. You will have a detailed physical description of her on your books, won't you?'

'Yes, Inspector. Of course we have.'

'Could you give me her height exactly?'

'Yes, of course. I have it here. She is five feet eight and a half inches tall.'

'Blue eyes?'

'Of course.'

'Did she have any distinguishing marks on her, such as an appendix scar or a scar following a mastoid operation, or a hysterectomy or a birthmark or anything like that?'

'No. No. Nothing unusual to identify here. But of course, she would be unmistakable. A face like hers . . . her features were unusual, classical . . . unique. I would recognize her anywhere.'

Angel hesitated. He was almost drawn into saying what he thought, but he managed to control himself. Good coppers ask questions but never volunteer information. Information is part of a policeman's stock in trade. And sometimes it is expensive to get hold of it.

'Have you found her?' Melanie asked. 'Has she been seen somewhere?'

'Not exactly,' he said, which might not have been the truth, but that was all he said.

'If you need someone to ID her from CCTV or something like that, I could do it.'

'Yes. Yes. Thanks very much. I'll let you know if it becomes necessary.'

He replaced the receiver. His face looked grim. If Melanie could see the body now, the body that he thought was Katrina's, maybe she wouldn't have offered to ID it so rashly.

There was a knock at the door. Crisp and Scrivens came in.

Angel turned to Scrivens first. 'Ted, I want you to go to the safe house and bring Gabriel Grainger here. Don't bring his wife. I just want him. All right?'

'Yes, sir.' He dashed off.

'Now, Trevor,' he said to Crisp. 'I need to find out if Chancey is back from wherever he went to yesterday, and confirmation that he spent the night at home and is in his office today as usual. You could go to his offices. He doesn't know you. You could tell the girl on reception you're looking for a job. Start from there. And there's a chambermaid works at the house. Her Christian name is Maria. You might be able to find out her full name. You'll like this job. She's very pretty. But there's a snag. I need to know that info today, so there's no time for any foreplay, just get on with it. All right?'

Crisp grinned. 'Yes, sir.'

He went out and closed the door.

It was a tall order, but Crisp had always been one for the ladies; he was gifted with the looks and the chat. And was the best on Angel's team at extricating info with ease and charm.

Angel picked up the phone and tapped in the Bromersley general hospital number. It was answered quickly and he asked for the mortuary. He was soon through.

'Good morning, Mac. I know it's early days, but what can you tell me?'

'Well, what do you want to know?'

'I want to ID the body, of course. Have you managed to have a look at it? Is it Katrina Chancey or somebody else? I've found out she's five feet eight and a half inches, blue eyes and no surgery or birthmarks.'

'Well, all that fits this corpse. I can close in on her age a bit. I'd say that she's between sixteen and twenty-five.'

'That helps. What about fingerprints?'

'No chance. Her hands were totally mutilated. As are her face and mouth, which also rules out ID by dental records.'

'He certainly made an excellent job of concealing her ID.'

'There's plenty of body parts: hair, skin, fluids for DNA.'

'Yeah. But we need something to compare it with. Anyway, thanks, Mac.'

'You're welcome.'

He replaced the phone. He rubbed his chin. Things were looking good. Everything pointed to the corpse being that of Katrina Chancey. But it would have to be proved positively before it could be legally accepted that indeed it was her. DNA was looking to be the only way. There was no knowledge of any family. Nobody knew anything about where she came from. Chancey wasn't likely to assist, even if he knew. Indeed, he had put everything in their way to make it impossible.

There was a knock at the door. It was Scrivens with the tall, handsome dark-haired womanizer, Gabriel Grainger. His arm was in a sling and there was a small sticking plaster above his left eyebrow. He was obviously going to be cagey. He looked sidelong at Angel.

'Thanks Ted,' Angel said.

Scrivens went out.

Angel nodded at Grainger, looked at the sling, pointed to a chair and they sat down.

'I haven't done anything wrong, Inspector. Not a thing, you know. You need to understand that.'

'How's the arm,' Angel said evenly.

'It's OK,' Grainger said with a shrug, then he winced. The movement produced pain the man hadn't expected.

Angel almost smiled.

'Tell me what happened on the night of Friday, the thirteenth of April. That was the night of the mysterious phone call, when you packed a suitcase and left Zoe.'

'I didn't leave Zoe in the way that you make it sound. It's all been very difficult. I've been unable to get a job for six months, you know. Everybody wants references. We've been living on dole money.'

'Yes, yes,' Angel said.

'Yes, well, a week or so before I left, I had answered an ad in the paper for a smart, young executive, over six feet, dark hair, good physique. I had all the qualifications for the job, and I was interviewed by Frank Chancey in his posh office at his big factory. He was offering three hundred quid a week. It was a short interview. He didn't ask many questions and he said he would consider me and let me know. I thought it was a brush-off. I had had so many. I was getting used to it, you know?'

Angel nodded.

'Anyway he rang up in a panic on that Friday night. He said he wanted to offer me the job and told me that it was all hush-hush. He said he wanted to buy the timber rights for a massive area in Cumbria, when they came up on offer. He wanted me to be placed in a strategic position, able to be the first to become aware of the rights coming on the market, and the first, maybe the only one, to put in a bid on his behalf. All I had to do was look as if I was on holiday, tell nobody I was there and ask no questions about timber. I was not to mention his name, because he was so well-known in the timber business he said it might interest other possible purchasers and thereby push up the price. At that money I naturally agreed. He said that he'd heard rumblings that this deal might be coming to a head very soon indeed. If I wanted the job, I was to pack a bag immediately that night, tell nobody and meet him at the end of the street in ten minutes. He would give me five hundred pounds and then send me three hundred pounds each week in folding money by registered post. He told me that there was a train leaving at ten o' clock for Leeds, then up to Penrith in Cumbria. Then it was about a half hour's ride by taxi to a little hotel called the King's Arms at Ridley Stewart. I agreed, of course. I was very enthusiastic about it. I told Zoe what I could earn, being a millionaire's representative. I thought it was the beginning of a break for me. Anyway, the hotel was in the middle of nowhere. I was comfortable enough, and he was paying the hotel bill, but bored out my skin. The following Tuesday I got another three hundred quid. I was rolling in it. I couldn't contact Zoe because I'd said that I wouldn't and I didn't want to stop the gravy train, now did I? I wasn't to know what was going to happen. Anyway, yesterday morning, I was in the hotel at Ridley Stewart. I had just come back in from a stroll to a petrol station along the road to buy a news-paper, when a big man in a clown's mask came in. He was waving a gun.'

'What time was this?'

'About twelve noon.'

'Yes. Go on. What did he say?'

'He didn't say anything. He opened the door. It wasn't locked. I was hanging up my raincoat in the wardrobe at the far side of the room. He fired the gun at me twice. It made a hell of a row. The first shot must have missed me: the second hit me in the arm. I feigned a stumble, and was dropping to the floor. There was a tray of dirty breakfast pots, a teapot and stuff on the bed. I grabbed at it, threw it at him then made straight for the bedroom window, barged through it, dropped about eight feet on to a garage roof, ran along it. The big man in the mask fired several shots after me, but he missed. I was petrified. I ran all the faster, lowered myself on to the gutter-ing and dropped the eight or ten feet to the floor. Then I ran like hell. I ran into the trees at the back of the hotel. There are plenty of them up there. Then I was wandering round for an hour or so until I came to a road. It was the main road. I started thumbing traffic. I thought nothing would ever stop, but a diesel tanker wagon did. Gave me a lift into Penrith.

Got to the train station. Fortunately I had my money-clip and wallet on me. Caught a train to Leeds, then home. The rest you know. I've been wondering what the man in the clown mask wanted, why he wanted me dead. He clearly did. What have *I* done?'

'Who knew you were there?'

Grainger looked up. 'Only Mr Chancey.'

* * *

'It's got to be Chancey, Ron. I asked Grainger who knew he was there, and he said only Mr Chancey.'

'Can we prove it, sir?'

Angel rubbed his chin. Suddenly he reached out to the phone and tapped in a number. 'Ahmed, find Ted Scrivens for me. He might be in the canteen.'

He replaced the phone and turned back to Gawber.

'Trevor Crisp said that he followed Chancey in a red Ferrari and eventually lost him. He couldn't keep up with him. That'll likely be the car he's supposed to have bought for Katrina.'

Angel suddenly had another idea. He picked up the phone and tapped in another number. He was ringing Crisp. It was soon answered. He asked him for the index number of Chancey's Ferrari. Crisp soon found it from his notebook. Angel wrote it on a pad in front of him and rang off.

There was a knock at the door. It was Scrivens. 'You wanted me, sir?'

'Ah, Ted. This is the index number of Chancey's Ferrari. I want you to go round to his garage at the side of Chancey House. It should be there. I want to know if we can place it anywhere in Cumbria yesterday. The milometer reading, the earth on the tread of the tyres. If we can, we can get him on the attempted murder of Gabriel Grainger. That would be the beginning of the end of Frank Chancey.'

Scrivens's eyes shone. 'I'll do what I can, sir,' he said and dashed out.

Angel turned to Gawber. He ran his hand through his hair. 'Look Ron, that body has no face, teeth or fingers. How do we possibly prove who it is? Her hair is the colour of Katrina's of course. The info that comes in both from Mac and her model agency exactly matches her description, but we still cannot prove it. All the evidence we have stacked up against him is useless unless we can prove that that body is incontrovertibly that of Katrina Chancey. The defence counsel would have a big laugh at us if we could only say it looks like her, but we can't prove it! Don't you see, that's what Chancey was all about? That's what all the changes to the house have been about. The five plumbers to change all the U bends, the washing down with bleach, repainting the woodwork, the new car, all her clothes to the cleaners or laundry, carpets cleaned. The thirty-six pairs of new shoes: of course the size didn't matter. The poor lass was never going to wear them anyway. Even her hairbrush had gone, supposedly in her luggage with her to Rome. Huh! We'll never see *that* again.'

His jaw dropped. 'I didn't realize.'

'Somehow, we have got to get Katrina's DNA. A single hair of Katrina's, from her clothes, from anywhere, that is definitely hers, and we can prove it's hers, that matches up with the dead body, and we've got him. But where can we get *that* from?'

SEVENTEEN

His office was quiet and still . . . like a sailing boat in a windless sea. It was the calm before the storm.

Angel's enthusiastic team were busy trying to ferret out the final link of evidence that was going to put Frank Chancey away for two murders and an attempted murder. All that was needed was the tiniest proven sample of Katrina Chancey's DNA.

There was nothing more that Angel could think of to do. If he had had the backing of his superintendent he could have obtained a search warrant and taken Chancey's study at his house and his office at his factory to pieces. There might, there just might have been something there that could have provided that vital DNA. Of course, the chief constable would have been against it, and Harker would have been against it. Angel wasn't surprised about the superintendent. He reckoned he was always against everything Angel wanted to do, and he wasn't up to another round with the honey monster at that time.

He rubbed his chin and looked at the pile of papers in front of him. He wasn't up to wading through that paper chase at that time, either. He turned away. His eye caught Peter Wolff's filing cabinet. He had hardly given it more than a cursory glance since finding the keys to Wolff's safe. He went over to it and pulled out the top drawer. The many files had names neatly written in alphabetical order. He pulled one out and took it to his desk. He looked carefully at it. Each file was labelled with a customer's name. It contained meticulous detail of the customer's requirements, wig size, colour requested, cost, source of materials, time making it, labour amount charged, total cost, total charged and date paid. Angel's eyebrows shot up. There seemed to be hundreds of files like that, some containing only a single sheet of paper. He rubbed his chin and ran his finger long the tabs of the files down the As and the Bs to the Cs . . . To Carter, Caspar, Chalfont, then Chancey. Chancey! He snatched out the file, took it over to his desk and began to read it. After a few moments his heart began to pound. There it was, in black and white.

'Got it!' he yelled. He looked up, sighed deeply, snatched up the phone and tapped in a number. He was trying to reach Gawber in the CID room. He wasn't there. He told Ahmed to find him before he went home. He tried him on his mobile.

The church clock in the distance chimed five o'clock.

There was a knock on his door. It was Gawber.

* * *

It was ten minutes to six.

Angel and Gawber were standing outside the main entrance to Chancey House, when Jimmy Lyle answered the door.

The little man was wearing an uncomfortable expression. 'I'll see if Mr Chancey will see you, but it is not his favourite time for receiving, you understand.'

Angel nodded. He knew that if Chancey wouldn't see him, he'd wait there and send Gawber back for a warrant.

They stood there waiting ten minutes before an irritable Frank Chancey came to the door. 'Now Angel, what's this all about? And who is that you've got there?'

Angel was seething. He didn't like being deliberately kept waiting, particularly by a man who was a murderer, a crook and a parasite. 'Good evening, Mr Chancey,' he said. 'This is DS Gawber. Can we have a few minutes of your very valuable time?'

'You'll have to make it quick. I have a social engagement in an hour and I have to get ready.'

'Perhaps we can have a word in your study?'

'What?' Chancey sighed noisily. 'Very well.'

They followed the tall, handsome figure through the hall, up the stairs, along the corridor to his study. When the three men were comfortably seated, and the door closed, Angel said, 'It was the change in the length of your wife's hair that gave me the clue I needed.'

Chancey blinked. 'What are you talking about?'

'Tragically, Mr Chancey, I know where your wife is. And she won't ever be coming back.'

'Of course she will,' Chancey snapped.

Angel's lips tightened against his teeth. 'No sir. You murdered your wife during a row, in the bedroom upstairs here in this house. It is not certain how, probably a blow to the head. You carried her body round next door, knowing that Lord Tiverton, his wife and their staff were away. You made sure that Katrina would not be identifiable by her dental records or her fingerprints, by brutally destroying her jaws and her finger and thumb ends; you did this on the jetty with a pane hammer. You pushed her into a suit of armour stolen from Lord Tiverton's outbuildings and wheeled her out to Tiverton's motorboat in a wheelbarrow. You dropped her inside the steel suit, into the middle of the lake.'

Chancey stared at him speechless.

'Then you set about covering up your tracks. I now know why you've had the house turned upside down, had everything cleaned, polished or changed, even to throwing away all her shoes and replacing them with new. It didn't matter that some of them weren't the right size, the poor woman wasn't ever going to wear any of them.

'You thought that, whatever evidence against you we might be able to obtain, no case could be brought against you if the victim could not be proved to be Katrina Chancey. So the house was scrubbed down, painted and polished, her clothes laundered, and so on, because you thought that you could destroy all traces of her, even her DNA. Without DNA or any distinguishing marks, you thought that the police wouldn't even be able to trace her. If they *were* able to find a dead body, there would be no possible way to prove it was her and thereby accuse you of murder. You remembered that Peter Wolff had bought some of her hair, and that he might still have some in stock, perhaps labelled with her name. So you burned every hair in the workshop and murdered him in the process, presumably because you couldn't possibly explain what you were doing. Murder him and he'd never talk. Destroy every hair in the place and nobody could find any of Katrina's DNA. The plan, in theory, was perfect.

'You even produced a fantasy scenario to explain her disappearance. You paid a handsome Romeo figure, Gabriel

Grainger, to disappear at the same time as you had murdered and hidden her body. Then you tried to start a rumour that the two had gone off together. What you didn't tell Grainger was that you had planned to murder him in due course so that he couldn't come back and destroy the fantasy, which would certainly have given you away.'

'This is all nonsense.'

'I can prove it. It was these photographs of your dear wife Katrina that gave me the clue,' he said, indicating the four walls of the study.

Chancey glanced round at them and smiled. 'Oh yes. A tad too exciting for you, Angel, weren't they?'

'I can take them or leave them, sir. The thing I want to draw your attention to is the length of her hair.'

'Very sensual, don't you think?'

'It's more than twelve inches long.'

'Eighteen inches, I would say.'

'But that photograph in your desk drawer . . . would you be kind enough to get it out for me, sir?'

Chancey snatched open the drawer and tossed the silver framed picture of Katrina roughly on to the desktop. It was fortunate that the glass did not break.

'Now *there*,' Angel said. 'Her hair is short. Very short.'

Chancey shrugged. 'What are you getting at?'

'I have been looking very closely through Peter Wolff's meticulously kept records that escaped the fire you started. They say that Mrs Chancey had her hair cut short on the second of April. And that the beautiful locks were subsequently made into a wig.'

'I know all about it,' he said sneeringly. 'I *should* know! Katrina was the most beautiful as well as the most expensive woman on this earth. Hell, I paid a thousand pounds for it! I *should* know.'

'But that wig wasn't made for her, though, Mr Chancey,' Angel said as he walked round the back of Chancey's chair.

'I don't know why you are making such a big thing of this, Angel,' Chancey snarled, trying to keep Angel in sight as he passed behind the chair.

'Because,' Angel said grandly, 'her hair was cut and dyed and trimmed and a wig was made by Peter Wolff at your wife's instructions especially for *you*.' With a flourish he leaned forward and boldly grabbed hold of Chancey's hair. The beautiful black wig came away in Angel's hand, leaving Chancey as bald as a polished newel post.

'And it was this one, wasn't it?' Angel said, waving the wig triumphantly.

Chancey jumped up. His face was as red as a judge's robe. His head was totally hairless and shone like a pink Belisha beacon.

'Give it here,' he bawled.

'This was the wig made from Katrina's hair,' Angel said. 'And one hair from this wig will be more than enough DNA to put you away for life.'

'Give it me, here,' Chancey cried. 'It's not true. It's all lies. I did it for Katrina.' He leaned out to Angel to try to snatch the wig back. But Angel had already stuffed it into an evidence bag and was sealing it.

'It's evidence now, sir,' he growled and turned to Gawber.

'I've got everything I need now, Ron. Cuff him, charge him with murder, and let's get off home.'

* * *

It was 8 o'clock when Angel arrived home. He was tired but quietly elated.

Mary wasn't pleased.

'Your dinner is ruined! Ruined! I don't know why I bother. You didn't even have the courtesy to ring and let me know.'

'I am sorry. But I was in the middle of a very complicated case. It just wasn't possible.'

'Sit down. I'll bring it through.'

'Very complicated. But we got Frank Chancey for murder.'

'There's some more gravy, but I still think it will be dry.'

'He murdered two people and attempted a third.'

'Be careful. The plate's hot. And it's my auction tonight, you know.'

'He came quietly though, after an initial show of outrage and innocence. He's not a nice man. He should get twenty years minimum.'

'Don't cover it in salt, Michael. It's bad for your heart!'

'You see, it was all a matter of DNA. It was very clever of him.'

'He said he would put it up early, before the punters had spent up. Better chance of getting a good price.'

'He might have got away with it, on a technicality.'

'I thought that was very good of him. I told him to make the point that even though it wasn't in the best condition, it was by Chippendale.'

'I'm not going to be too popular with the chief constable. He was a friend of Chancey. In the Masons, I think. Went drinking together.'

'There's strawberries and ice cream to follow. At least that wasn't ruined. I'll fetch the ice cream. It will be softening.'

'Of course, it'll be an embarrassment to Harker.' Angel grinned. 'He always does exactly what the chief tells him to do, regardless. He hasn't the guts to stand up to him.'

'So his wife, Edna Williamson said she'd ring me and let me know what it'd fetched when she got a moment. She does the money side of it. Records the bids, takes in the money, knocks off their percentage and pays out when the auction is over. Is that enough ice cream? She should be ringing any time now.'

'The job would be all right if it wasn't for Harker.'

'I've sweetened them, love. I don't think you'll want any more sugar.'

The phone rang.

Mary stiffened. She stood up. Her face looked like the condemned woman going to the scaffold.

'Who's that ringing at this time?' Angel said.

'It's all right. It'll be for me.'

She went out of the room in a trance. She picked up the phone tentatively.

Angel was enjoying the fish pie, if that was what it was. Although it was a bit dry. A knob of butter would be nice.

He strained to hear whether the call was for him. He hoped there wasn't any difficulty at the station that might need his attention. It was a quarter past eight and he didn't want to turn out. He reckoned it must have been for Mary or she would have come back or called him. He suddenly heard a little scream, then she said something very loudly; she was excited or distressed.

He put down his knife and fork and looked at the hall door. He couldn't make out what was happening. There were a few more exchanges, then she replaced the phone. She didn't come into the room immediately. Angel was curious to know what was happening.

Eventually she came through with a forced smile on her face.

He knew her better than anybody. Something unusual had happened. But he didn't understand.

'What was that all about?' he said.

Mary's eyes were strange. She looked as if she was in another world. She didn't reply.

'Who was that?' he said. 'What's happened?'

Eventually, in a monotone, she said, 'The auctioneer put up the table, my Chippendale table, and he didn't get a bid. Not a single bid. He tried to get it started, but it was no good. I don't believe it.'

Angel wrinkled his nose but said nothing. He'd known it was rubbish when he first saw it at Seymour Timms's ramshackle place. He had written the £500 off the moment he saw the damned thing.

'But he put up the old books separately,' she continued, 'and one of the books was *Aesop's Fables*, an early edition with hand painted illustrated plates. There were two dealers in and, to cut a long story short, it was sold for six thousand pounds.'

Angel swallowed. 'How much?' he spluttered.

THE END

THE JOFFE BOOKS STORY

We began in 2014 when Jasper agreed to publish his mum's much-rejected romance novel and it became a bestseller.

Since then we've grown into the largest independent publisher in the UK. We're extremely proud to publish some of the very best writers in the world, including Joy Ellis, Faith Martin, Caro Ramsay, Helen Forrester, Simon Brett and Robert Goddard. Everyone at Joffe Books loves reading and we never forget that it all begins with the magic of an author telling a story.

We are proud to publish talented first-time authors, as well as established writers whose books we love introducing to a new generation of readers.

We won Trade Publisher of the Year at the Independent Publishing Awards in 2023 and Best Publisher Award in 2024 at the People's Book Prize. We have been shortlisted for Independent Publisher of the Year at the British Book Awards for the last five years, and were shortlisted for the Diversity and Inclusivity Award at the 2022 Independent Publishing Awards. In 2023 we were shortlisted for Publisher of the Year at the RNA Industry Awards, and in 2024 we were shortlisted at the CWA Daggers for the Best Crime and Mystery Publisher.

We built this company with your help, and we love to hear from you, so please email us about absolutely anything bookish at feedback@joffebooks.com.

If you want to receive free books every Friday and hear about all our new releases, join our mailing list here: www.joffebooks.com/freebooks.

And when you tell your friends about us, just remember: it's pronounced Joffe as in coffee or toffee!